TRUTH AND TEMPTATION

JULIA JARRETT

Dear readers,

Please note as a minor content warning, there is mention of the death of a family member 12 years prior to the story by cancer, and one character is admitted to the emergency room.

CONTENTS

Chapter One

Wyatt

"Trust me, I want nothing more than to be on a plane to St. Thomas right now. But I've got to get through the new store opening first. That *is* sort of my job, you know." I tuck my phone between my ear and my shoulder as I unlock the front door to my parents' vacation house. On the other end of the phone is my best friend from college, Jacob, who's been after me for weeks to join him at the Indigo Royal Resort in the Virgin Islands.

"Yeah, yeah, Mister Hot Shot Director of Expansion and Acquisitions." I can hear Jacob's eyes roll even over the phone. "Look, my man, you know next month is gonna be shit for you mentally. So why not spend some time with sun, sand, and beautiful women? C'mon Wyatt." His voice is cajoling, and the sound of laughter and music in the background doesn't help. He's got a valid point, and a big part of me seriously wants to say fuck it to responsibility and go. But the permanent weight of guilt on my conscience holds me in place like an anchor dragging me down.

"I know. Look man, if everything goes smoothly, I'll try to get down there after the grand opening. Talk later, okay? I need to unpack."

It's not often that I'm grateful for the superficial trappings of wealth my family is fortunate enough to have access to. But right now, walking into a house that no one has been in for months, yet still having it warm, clean, and, I know, full of food is a relief. I'm exhausted, having flown the red eye from Toronto all the way to Vancouver. I was in back-to-back meetings about some of the new bookstores our family company, Crawford Books, has opened on the East Coast. Once in Vancouver, I checked in with my parents briefly, only to then grab a chartered sea plane over to Vancouver Island, and finally make the drive to Dogwood Cove.

My parents bought this house when I was young, to use as a summer home. Mom tried to call it a cottage, but any place that has three bedrooms, a gourmet kitchen, a gas fireplace, a hot tub, and a view of the ocean can't be called a cottage, if you ask me. Regardless, this place has always been a refuge for my family. It's in a small town, but from what I remember, the place is big on personality. The quiet pace is relaxing, and growing up, my brother and I loved boogie boarding at the beach and hiking in the forest.

The usual ache hits me, just as it does every time I think of Ryder. Losing a family member is never easy. Losing a twin? A lot fucking worse.

After dumping my bags in the bedroom I plan on using for the week or so I'm in town, I head to the kitchen. Sure enough, the fridge is stocked, courtesy of the property management company my parents hire to watch the place. I throw together a sandwich, pour a glass of water, and sit down at the breakfast bar. Opening my computer, I scan my inbox to see if there's anything pressing at work I need to deal with.

At the risk of sounding like a spoiled, entitled rich kid, I'm stuck in a job that I wish I didn't have and feel like I don't deserve. It should have been Ryder in the role, not me. He is — was — the business-minded one of us. I hated wearing a tie, and being stuck indoors was torture. But when he died from cancer twelve years ago, I had no choice but to step up and into his unfillable shoes. The harsh truth I face everyday is that he's not here, and I am. Which means the close to one hundred emails staring at me are mine to deal with.

With a deep breath, and a long pull from my drink, I get to work weeding through everything. An hour later, the unread emails are down to just ten that I have to address, with another twenty sent off to my assistant to be handled. I hate being tied to a screen like this, interacting over emails and phone calls.

Stretching my arms overhead, I shut down my computer and stand to clean up from lunch as my phone rings. Glancing at the call display, I know I have to answer.

"Hey, Mom."

"Hi, honey, did you make it to the house okay?"

It doesn't matter that I'm a thirty-six-year-old man who hasn't lived at home for almost half my life, my mother will always — without fail — call to check up on me when I travel.

"Yeah, I'm here, just going through my emails. Do you know if Dad saw the one from the team in Calgary? I'm thinking we'll need someone out there soon."

"I'm sure he's looked at it." My mother's tone turns chiding. "You need to get some sleep, Wyatt. I can hear how tired you are."

"I know, but I still haven't totally adjusted to the time change. I'm gonna try to get a nap later, but I need to finish answering a few of these." I take another sip of water and stare out the kitchen window. It's early afternoon, but I've been up for over twenty-four hours now and I can feel it seeping through my bones.

"Wyatt..."

I silently curse. I know what she's about to ask. Every fall, we go through this. Honestly, I'm surprised she waited until October to ask for the first time this year. Normally, she starts trying to convince me to come home for the anniversary of Ryder's death much earlier.

"Do you think you could come home next month? I'd really like to be together as a family this year."

"I don't know, Mom."

"Okay, sweetheart." Her voice betrays her, letting me know she's hurting. I mentally add it to the mountain of guilt I'm always carrying. "Well, we'll see you in a week at the opening in Westport. Let us know if you need anything before then, but I'm sure you'll have everything running perfectly by the time we get there."

"You bet, Mom. See you soon."

"I love you, Wyatt."

"Love you, too." My voice sounds hollow, at least to me it does. We hang up and my head falls to the cold marble counter. I hate upsetting my mother. But work has no room for remorse. Lifting my head and blinking away the deep feeling of fatigue, I return my attention to the emails waiting for me.

Sometimes it fucking sucks being Wyatt Crawford.

After two hours of conference calls dealing with a situation at one of our stores in Alberta that is moving to a new location, I'm finally done with the time sensitive work I had to deal with for Crawford Books. Every muscle in my back aches when I stand up and stretch. I need to find somewhere close by to get some rock climbing in. My mind needs the distraction of focusing on nothing more than the rock face and figuring out my next hold, and my body needs the sensation of stretching to its utter limit before proving how much more I'm capable of.

An interviewer for some society magazine once asked me why I enjoy so many activities that are deemed "risky." They tried to paint me as some reckless rich kid with no respect for my own mortality. I laughed it off at the time, but it was actually chilling how close to the truth they were.

Losing my twin to an aggressive cancer that no amount of money could cure made me look at things differently. I realized it doesn't matter what the fuck I do — when it's my time, it's my time. So why not live my life to the fullest extreme and ignore any fears or worries that I might be pushing things too far.

When you layer in the suffocation I constantly feel from having to step into Ryder's shoes at the company and set aside my own plans and dreams, yeah, you could say I don't hold back when it comes to extracurriculars. Sometimes, the only moments I feel like I can truly breathe are when I'm paragliding over the ocean or skiing down a double black diamond.

Opening the texting app on my phone, I fire off a message to Jacob. He's from Vancouver Island, so if anyone is going to know somewhere to rock climb, it'll be him.

WYATT: Hey where's a good place to climb around here? I'm gonna go crazy if I don't get outside soon.

JACOB: There are better ways to release all that pent-up energy my man...

I roll my eyes at his not so subtle innuendo. It's exactly the kind of one-liner he likes to throw at me whenever he thinks I'm heading down a dark path.

WYATT: Right. And I'm on a work trip, not looking for a girlfriend

JACOB: Who said anything about a girlfriend?! I'm just pointing out that getting laid might make the trip a hell of a lot more enjoyable. How long has it been, anyway? Was it Marika in Mexico?

WYATT: The fact that you keep track of my sex life is disturbing.

JACOB: Well someone's gotta make sure you don't go so long you forget how to use your dick.

WYATT: Thanks. I think. So back to my question — where can I climb?

An hour later, I'm locking the door behind me, having arranged for my climbing gear to be shipped overnight from my apartment in Vancouver. Hopefully, it's here in time for me to head out tomorrow, after I go to Westport and check on how things are going at the store in preparation for the opening.

Fall on the West Coast is fucking incredible, when it's not raining, that is. The leaves are changing, it's cool and crisp, but not too cold, and there's a relaxed feel in the air. Then again, compared to Toronto or Vancouver, any time of year on the island feels relaxed.

The neighborhood is full of older homes, but they've all been maintained really well. Swing sets are in the front yards, and the few people who are outside all wave or smile as I walk past. The fresh air is helping to keep my exhaustion at bay, but I'm in need of something stronger. Here's hoping Dogwood Cove is big enough to sustain a Starbucks, although I don't remember seeing one on my drive in.

The downtown hasn't changed much. Low buildings line a quiet street that wraps around a square grass area with a gazebo in the middle. It's like something out of a cheesy movie. A glance around doesn't reveal the familiar green and white sign that is a beacon to coffee addicts everywhere, but I do notice something else that's different.

A bookstore.

The name on the awning is Pages, and underneath it says *Bibliophiles Welcome*. Catchy. Just next to it is another new business, and my mouth instantly starts to water.

The Nutty Muffin Bakery boasts a handwritten sign out front, stating *Apple nut muffins — two for one, today only*. Sounds good to me. I push open the door, surprised at just how busy it is for the time of day. Almost every seat is taken and there's a short line waiting to order. I join the lineup and take out my phone to scroll through some news headlines while I wait.

"All I'm saying is, the reviews on it are mind-blowing. It might help you!" The loudly teasing voice comes from behind me.

"Serena, could you please refrain from talking about intimate products in public?"

A grin stretches across my face at the obviously disapproving response. Whoever said it was trying to be more discreet, but I'm close enough to hear anyway. I want to turn around, but something tells me my contribution to whatever the conversation is about might not be welcome.

"Paige. Relax. No one knows we're talking about B.O.B's."

I tense my shoulders to stop from laughing. *I'm starting to get an idea...*

"Regardless. This is inappropriate conversation for a place of business."

Now I'm really curious to see who speaks so formally. The voice doesn't sound old, just old-fashioned, I guess you could say. Suddenly, a pretty brunette comes out from behind the counter. "What are you two doing waiting back there? Sebastian has your stuff up front." She flashes me a quick smile. "Sorry, sir. We'll be right with you.

I lift my shoulders in acquiescence as she turns and walks back to the front counter, followed by two other women who must be the intimate product ladies. One is petite, with long blonde hair, the other is taller, also with long hair, only hers is a bit darker, with a slight red hint to it. I missed seeing their faces because I was staring at my phone, trying not to be too obvious with my checking them out. But judging by their outfits, I can tell that the taller one is Miss Old-Fashioned. Blondie is decked out in colourful leggings, some filmy sort of wrap skirt, and a tight-fitting sweater, whereas the other one is in black pants and a light collared shirt, with a cardigan on top.

Now that their backs are to me, I watch the women interact with the male barista at the front as he hands them two reusable cups. There's a familiarity to their interactions, making it clear they're regular customers. The brunette from earlier comes out from what I assume is the kitchen area and hands them each a paper bag.

"There's lunch and a muffin. Paige, did that paperback copy of *Heartbeat* come in yet? I'm dying to read it," she asks, and like a lightning bolt, a connection forms in my head.

Paige, Pages, books.

The irony of everything is not lost on me. Here I am, the wealthy heir to a bookstore chain fortune, standing in a small-town coffee shop, eavesdropping on a conversation about vibrators or dildos, if I'm not mistaken, between a prim and proper bookstore owner and her friend.

The women turn to leave and I finally get a glimpse of their faces. My eyes travel over blondie, or I guess Serena is her name, categorically noticing her attractiveness. Then I land on Paige, and *fuck*.

Freckles.

She has freckles.

A slight upturned nose, large dark-rimmed glasses, a perfect heart-shaped mouth, and freckles.

No one except Ryder ever knew that fucking freckles were so goddamn attractive to me. I can't explain it, it's weird and random and probably laughable, but a woman with freckles is gorgeous to me. Maybe it has to do with natural beauty versus created beauty, although, don't get me wrong, a woman wearing a face of makeup, looking glamourous is stunning as well. Either way, freckles have always been my undoing. Especially if they're on more

than just her face...

Neither one of them spare me a glance as they walk past, which shouldn't bother me, but for some reason I don't want to explore right now, it does.

"Alrighty, what I can get for you?" I look up to the bright-faced young man behind the counter. His name tag reads *Sebastian* and he's got a welcoming smile on his face.

"Americano misto and I guess I'll try an apple nut muffin, please."

He tilts his head to the side. "Oh trust me, there is no 'I guess' about it. You need an apple nut muffin, and today's your lucky day. Mila made extra."

I nod and give him a small smile in return. I have no idea who Mila is, or why these muffins are so important, but okay. He rings me up, hands me a bag holding the famous muffin, and directs me to wait over to the side for my coffee.

Just a few minutes later, I'm walking out the door of the café, and somehow my feet automatically turn to the left and carry me to the purple door of Pages. I'm not one to hesitate, more of an *act now, think later* kind of guy, so I'm pushing open the door before I can think twice about it.

There are bells attached to the door that make a surprisingly pleasant sound when I enter. Inside, it's warm and inviting. Not too crowded with shelves, but full of enough books that it's easy to see the appeal of the smaller store. My marketing eye travels over the shelves, taking in the unique categories she has things divided into. In what I assume is the mystery section, I see *Crimes Solved by Professionals* next to *Crimes Solved by Cats*. On another shelf, there's *Here There Be Dragons* and on another — a shelf filled with books on politics — I see a label that makes me laugh out loud. *Fiction Masquerading as Truth*. I take note of a couple of seating areas, including one that is beside what I assume is a gas fireplace, and another with giant pillows in bright colours on the floor, perfectly situated in the children's section.

"Can I help you find something?"

I turn to see Paige standing to the side, a stack of books in her arms. Her brow furrows with a slight frown. "You were in front of us at the café."

"Ah, yes." Shit, does she know I overheard her conversation? I open my mouth to apologize, but then she continues.

"I meant to apologize for Mila serving us ahead of you. She does not always consider the optics of such a decision in front of customers who are unaware of our close friendship."

Her direct and formal speech pattern intrigues me. It's refreshing in a way; there's no pretense to what she says, and I can appreciate that. I watch as she places the books on a shelf under another category sign that has me laughing under my breath *Books that Could Be a PowerPoint*.

"Do people still use PowerPoint?"

Paige pauses in her shelving, turning to me with a copy of the latest from a popular self-help guru in hand. "Excuse me?"

I gesture to the sign. She looks up, then back to me, her lips quirking up in a smile. "I'm not entirely certain, to be honest."

She places the last book on the shelf and turns to face me, extending her hand. "I'm
Paige. Do you need a book?"

I place my hand in hers, surprised by the firmness to her shake. "Wyatt. And doesn't everyone need a book?"

Her eyes widen. "I certainly think so."

Chapter Two

Paige

Firm handshake, smooth-skinned palms, warm. I notice these things subconsciously, my mind filing them away. Taking in the sensation of his hand in mine, I analyze my reaction. It's...enjoyable, feeling his skin against mine. Odd. I don't believe I've felt that way from a handshake before.

"...guidebooks for the area, something that includes information on climbing routes."

His deep voice jolts me back to the present moment. Another odd experience. Normally, I'm capable of maintaining focus on multiple subjects, but I truly lost track of what he was saying. I am quite disconcerted by what's happening to me right now. Thankfully, my brain catches up with what he's saying relatively quickly, and I'm able to formulate an adequate reply.

"Yes, I have multiple selections that may suit your needs." I pull my hand away from his, feeling a mild sense of loss when our palms lose contact. I walk over to the *How to Be A Local* section and quickly find the two books I'm thinking of before venturing close to him again and handing them over.

While he scans the cover and reads the descriptions, I surreptitiously catalogue more observations about the man in front of me. Tall, dark hair a touch too long and unruly, as if he's overdue for a haircut. Strong features with thick eyebrows that frame dark blue eyes, and an angular jawline, covered in what Serena would undoubtedly call 'scruff,' but is more accurately described as closely trimmed facial hair. He's attractive. An indescribable feeling starts to build inside my chest. I examine it critically, while still paying some attention to Wyatt. My breathing pattern is slightly rapid, but not constricted, meaning this is not an asthma flare up. After close to thirty years of dealing with my chronic illness, I am somewhat of an expert in the matter. So why do I feel my heart rate also accelerating?

Is this...desire?

Do I desire this complete stranger?

As quickly as that random thought flashes through my mind, I dismiss it. I have long since accepted that my body does not operate in the usual fashion when it comes to hormones, lust, and desire. I can appreciate an attractive man, such as Wyatt, but I have no urge to see or do more with anyone. As the colloquialism goes, been there tried that. And it was overall, anticlimactic. Pun intended.

Once I'm behind the counter, with some distance between myself and this bizarre sensation, I take a deep calming breath, feeling my lungs expand and retract with the familiar rhythm brought on by years of breath control work. "Are you in town long?" I ask, making polite conversation as any professional business owner would.

It's perfectly acceptable and normal that my eyes follow him as he walks over and places the two books that I suggested to him onto the counter in front of me. At least, that is what I tell myself.

"A week or so."

Not long then. That's good. It's uncomfortable for me, this feeling I have. I don't understand — why now, why him? Why is this previously dormant part of my body stirring to life, like a bear coming out of a long hibernation?

When I look up from placing his books in a bag, I blink to make sure I'm not mistaken. Wyatt is staring at me, his eyes seeming to map a pattern across my face. I see his gaze linger on my nose, a strange place for him to focus on, to be certain. The uncomfortable feeling in me deepens. He's likely noticing all of my freckles. I refuse to waste time and energy on being self-conscious, but I am aware of them, aware that they are one more way in which I am different from the status quo.

I push the bridge of my glasses up my nose. "Will that be all?" Serena is always telling me to not sound so formal, but right now it can't be helped. I need to put some space between my confusing reaction and the man causing it.

All I get is an enigmatic smile in return, and a rap of his knuckles on the counter before Wyatt turns and saunters toward the door. With one hand on the handle, he pauses, and looks over his shoulder at me.

"It was a pleasure to meet you, Paige."

I wish I could say the same, yet the overwhelming emotion tumbling around inside of me is not pleasure. It's confusion.

Thankfully, the rest of the day passes uneventfully. I make some more sales and spend some time organizing a signing I have next month with an author from Vancouver. After the store closes for the evening comes my favourite ritual. My Nan is the one who inspired me to open a bookstore, and the start-up money came from the inheritance she left me. She fostered my love of books, and we spent many evenings listening to Joni Mitchell and reading together. Now, that music is my companion each evening, and the small ritual helps me feel connected to the woman who gave me the gift of a love of books.

With the music playing softly through the speakers, I wander the shelves, tidying, restocking, and simply running my hands over the spines of my books as if they were old friends. Which, in a way, they are. Books have long been my safe harbour, my escape, my way to experience the world without ever leaving Vancouver Island. So many of my days and nights were spent alone in hospital beds, hooked up to nebulizers and oxygen machines while asthma wreaked havoc on my lungs, with only my books to keep me company.

As soon as I was old enough to advocate for myself, I requested my parents not stay with me during overnight stays. My mom's level of anxiety and worry was too high for me to handle, and my father was uncomfortable in any healthcare setting. To tell the truth, I don't think either of them minded when I first said I didn't need them to stay, although, for a while, it did make Mom hover all the more closely when I would first return home after a hospital stay.

It's all I've ever known, this life of constantly being on alert for germs and other things that might trigger an episode.

Severe reactive airway disease.

Also known as viral-induced asthma, with the added personal triggers of allergies to cigarette smoke and some artificial perfumes.

After so many years with this disease, I have established a consistent management regime, with regular medications and inhalers, and preventative measures, such as controlled exercise and caution when it comes to environmental triggers. It doesn't always work — at least once or twice a year my respirologist in Victoria has to adjust my medications, but in general, I manage.

But the invisible scars of a life with chronic illness remain. I am all too aware that my social skills are lacking at times, that I don't pick up on cues and communication the way others do. That when I am with other people my speech comes across as more formal than necessary, courtesy of some deep-seated social anxiety. Homeschooled my entire childhood, my social circle consisted of my parents, my grandmother, and the other children in our homeschool cohort. None of us were the most outgoing of children, and even still, I was the odd one out with how often I missed group activities and outings, thanks to my asthma. The only travel I did was for doctor appointments. My world was small, safe, and sheltered. The boldest move I ever made was leaving my parents' home in Victoria and moving to Dogwood Cove. Living your life this way is a mindset that is not easy to shake, and while I certainly do more now than I ever did when I was younger, I still exercise cautious deliberation with every decision and action.

I finish my tidying of the shop just as Nana's favourite Joni Mitchell song comes on — "Both Sides, Now." My hips start to sway to the sultry sounds coming through the speaker. If Serena, a former ballerina and current dance teacher, saw me, she would never let me hear the end of it. But I can't possibly dance in front of anyone else. This is for me, and only me. Moving my body freely reminds me that I'm alive, and that despite the adversity bestowed upon me, I am still here. It's also the only time I feel truly connected to my body. So often I am at war with the physical side of me, begging it to breathe, to function, to allow me to do normal things. But moments like this, when I feel every movement, filling my soul with happiness, I am at peace with who I am.

At the last second before locking up, I remember to grab the book Mila is waiting for. As I turn the key in the door handle, my phone starts to ring in my purse. It takes me a moment to find it, breathing slowly against the chill in the air.

"Hello, Serena."

"Hey, girly! You done at the store?" Serena is the person I am closest to out of our group, despite the fact that we are quite different. She is bold, confident, beautiful, and outgoing. Everything I have accepted I will never be.

"Yes, I've just locked up."

"Excellent. So listen, I was talking with Mila and Ashley, and we've decided that the next book club is also gonna be a Pleasure Party!"

I stumble, and not from stepping awkwardly. "Excuse me?"

"You heard me, girly. Look, what you said at the winery opening has me worried. No woman should ever miss out on the joy of orgasms. And I'm willing to bet that you're your own worst enemy. You know I love you, but you have *got* to loosen up. If a few toys are the way to get you there, well, no shame in the sex toy game!"

"Serena, I appreciate your concern for my…wellbeing, but this is entirely unnecessary." My footsteps quicken; I'm anxious to get home and not have this conversation where someone may overhear. For that matter, I would rather not have this conversation at all, but Serena is nothing, if not tenacious.

"Paige. I'm serious. We need to fix this. You need orgasms."

I truly don't think I've ever heard such a solemn tone to Serena's voice. It's almost enough to make me take her seriously. "As I said previously, I'm sure I have experienced one, it just wasn't quite as breathtaking as it was for you. That's all. I felt the flush of warmth, nothing more. I don't feel as though I'm missing out on anything."

"And that is an atrocity. A woman's sexual pleasure is a thing to celebrate, not hide from!"

Oh dear, she's getting louder. I can only hope Serena isn't somewhere public, although knowing her, she's still at her dance studio getting caught up on the paperwork side of her job.

"Anyway, it's decided. Next book club, Mila knows a lady from Westport who's coming over to show us a bunch of different toys and accessories. And as your best friend —" Serena pauses for effect and my stomach turns in dread "— I plan on buying your first toy."

"Could we please discuss this further before any purchases are made?"

"Come on, Paige, why are you so resistant to this?" Exasperation laces her tone, and I feel a rush of guilt. She's only trying to help, I know.

"I'm sorry. I don't mean to be resistant, I just don't see this as warranting such a priority. I've never felt the need to experience personal pleasure, nor have I ever felt a strong enough desire for another individual to warrant exploring intimacy and sexual release any more than I already have. You would be wasting your money."

The phone line is silent for so long, I almost wonder if we were disconnected.

"I don't know why you think you aren't a sexual being, or that you don't need or deserve to enjoy your body and yourself in every possible way. It isn't true. You think you're content, that you don't need anyone or anything else in your life, but I don't believe that. I know you, Paige. Probably better than you realize I do. And I know that you need to feel loved. Physically *and* emotionally."

This time, the silence comes from me. There are occasions in which Serena is a remarkably insightful woman, and this is one of them. Before I can formulate a response, she continues.

"It's like I said at the winery. Someday, Paige, a guy is going to come along and sweep you off your feet. He'll make you realize that a woman as beautiful, intelligent, kind, and all-around amazing as you are deserves to be worshipped."

It's only much later, after I have eaten dinner, taken a shower, and climbed into bed that I allow myself to admit something slightly disconcerting.

The face that came to my mind the instant Serena said a guy would come along and sweep me off my feet was that of a virtual stranger. A man I may never see again. A man whose last name I don't even know.

He's also the only man I have met thus far in my life to ever stir feelings of what I can now acknowledge were likely the beginnings of attraction and lust.

Wyatt.

CHAPTER THREE

Wyatt

A light breeze blows past, ruffling my hair that is in desperate need of a haircut...ideally before the damn store opening in three days. Blowing my breath out on a slow exhale I push thoughts of work aside and focus on the environment around me. Thank fuck for waterproof hiking shoes because the trail is wet, small rivulets running everywhere from the heavy rain we had yesterday. Typical west coast fall. The tall trees that surround me reach up to the sky, allowing dappled sunlight reach me. I may have traveled the world in search of my next thrill, but nothing quite compares to the beauty of the forests here in British Columbia.

When I finally reach the end of the trail — on top of a bluff that overlooks all of Dogwood Cove and out to the ocean beyond — I find a dry patch of rock and sink down. The only sounds I hear are birds chirping and my own heavy breathing. In this moment I feel at peace. Nothing exists, no pressure, no guilt, no responsibilities. Just me and nature.

But that peace can't last forever. The hike down doesn't take very long, and all too soon I'm loading my pack into the back of my car. The bark of a dog has me looking up to see Paige walking into the parking lot from the opposite direction. A large dog walks beside her. She's not looking in my direction, but the dog notices me right away and its tail starts to wag.

"Is he yours?" I call out, instantly regretting it when she stumbles in surprise at my voice. "Sorry. I didn't mean to scare you." I wait until she's closer, then close the distance between us, holding my hand out for the dog to sniff. I can feel the force of Paige's gaze as I give the dog some attention.

"No, Milo is my friend's dog. I bring him with me for a walk sometimes. As company and bear protection."

My mouth curves up in a smile at her straightforward answer.

"Smart." A beat of silence passes between us. "I didn't see you up at the bluffs. Did you take a different trail?"

"No, I didn't do the bluffs trail. I was just walking along the flat path that goes to the river. The bluffs are more intense than I can usually handle."

I wouldn't exactly call the hike I just did intense, but I guess that just proves my point. Paige is nothing like any of the women I normally associate with. Sure, she's attractive, of course. Those damn freckles are there, even under her flush of exertion. And I like this more laid-back look. Her hair is a bit messy, her clothes are more casual. Gone is the collared shirt and tailored pants, and in their place are leggings that hug her slim curves and a tank top that shows a hint of cleavage. But she's quiet. Reserved.

I can't exactly see her going skydiving in Moab with me if she can't even handle a short hike.

"Are you finished with your observation of me?"

My eyes dart forward when she turns to face me and heat rushes to the surface of my skin. "Sorry, what?"

"You were looking at me quite intently, I assume you are forming some sort of observation or analysis of my appearance. Are you done?" She tilts her head to the side and I can't help but laugh. But when her lips turn down in a frown, I stop.

"I'm sorry. I was not intending that to be amusing. I misread social cues at times."

"No, Paige, I'm sorry, I shouldn't have laughed." I run my hands through my already messy hair. Shit, how do I get myself out of this? Taking my cue from her tendency to speak clearly, I opt for honesty. "Truthfully, I was a little embarrassed that you caught me looking at you."

"Why?"

"Jesus, you don't hold back, do you?" I know that's also not the right response by the downturn of her eyes. "Sorry. Shit. I keep putting my foot in my mouth around you."

"Did you know that saying originated from the early 1900s and is a play on the concept of having foot-and-mouth disease, which results in ulcers around your mouth and hands?"

This time I grin. "I did not know that, and now that I do, I don't think I'll ever use that saying again. Thanks for the education." I wink at her so she knows I'm teasing. At least, I hope she picks up on that. The truth is, I've spent my life surrounded by women who care more about appearance and pretense than real life. Talking to someone who is so literal, so straightforward, is refreshing. And challenging.

Paige is still looking uncertain, about me or about herself, I'm not exactly sure. Either way, I hate that I've made her doubt herself in any way. I'm intrigued by her, far more than I should be, seeing as I'm not staying in town long. Not to mention, her beauty aside, she is wrong for me on so many levels. Paige screams *long-term* and *commitment*. And I don't do either. By all rights, I should keep distance between us. But I don't want to.

"I was looking at you because you're beautiful."

Her eyes narrow, and I shrug. "You asked."

Paige looks down before lifting her gaze to me again.

"What brought you to Dogwood Cove, Wyatt?"

I'm not surprised she's changing the subject; it doesn't take a genius to realize Paige doesn't love talking about herself. But of all the things she could say, that right there is the one question I didn't want her to ask. I don't want her to know who I am. Something tells me she might not be interested in talking with someone whose company has the ability — if not the desire — to shut a store like hers down. Not that we would, but I suspect Paige is someone who plays it safe. In business and in life. Thinking quickly, I answer with what I wish I was here to do, instead of the truth.

"I want to start up an outdoor tourism company, and this part of the island seemed like a good spot. My family used to come here a lot when I was younger." There. That's not a lie, not exactly.

She makes a noncommittal sound. I'm not sure what it means. "You should speak with my friend Summer. She runs the Oceanside Resort and could be a beneficial partner for you in your business."

"Thanks, I'll do that." Fuck, this all feels forced and stilted. My normal charm is nonexistent around her. I guess some part of me knows it won't have any effect. "So, aside from running a bookstore and walking other people's dogs, what else do you enjoy doing?" God, I sound like a pathetic schmuck. But I'll try anything to keep this woman talking to me for a little while longer. I find myself fascinated by her, even after only two short interactions, this one included.

"I...I read to children admitted to the hospital in Westport."

My heart stutters at her quiet response. "That's amazing." But this conversation isn't. Paige has a tough shell that is proving to be hard to crack. Me being me, that only makes me more determined to get her comfortable with me, somehow.

I never was one to shy away from a challenge. Yet, something tells me pushing her too far out of her comfort zone won't work in my favour. Closing the trunk of my car, I shove my hands in my pockets. "Well. I need a shower." Damn, did her eyes just flare wider? "Maybe I'll see you around." This time I know I'm not mistaken when I see her lick her lips.

Huh. Interesting.

I don't bother checking my phone until I get home in an effort to delay my return to normal life as long as possible. But when I finally do, I see text messages waiting for me on my phone from Jacob, and from my dad. Opening Jacob's first, I laugh at the photo. He's got his arms around two very beautiful women and they're all smiling at me.

JACOB: This is what you're missing out on, man. Get your ass down to St Thomas.

My mind flashes to Paige. She's more alluring to me than either of those two women, which surprises me. She's a woman who undoubtedly requires a lot of work to get close to, which is the absolute opposite of my normal choice. Not one for commitment, I keep my relationships short and sweet, with the expectations clear from the outset. But I can't deny there's something about her that draws me in. Makes me curious to peel back the protective layers she's covered herself with.

WYATT: Stop rubbing it in. I'll see where things are at after the opening.

Can't avoid it anymore, duty calls. I switch over to the message from my father.

DAD: I just spoke with Laurel. She said the catering is lined up for Saturday. The soft opening for staff and publishing houses is set for ten, then we open to the public at one. Are you ready on your end?

WYATT: Yes. I've been in contact with Laurel as well. We've got three reps from local publishers coming, and Laurel is working on lining up some authors to come for signings within the first few months as well. I think this one will go well.

DAD: Excellent. And how are you settling in, is everything okay at the house?

His switch to a personal question makes me pause. After Ryder's death, Dad and I drifted apart. He knows I blame myself in some part for how everything ended for my brother, and I've always suspected he blames me, too. Not that he would ever come out and say it. Which makes it perfectly fine with me that we tend to keep our relationship focused on work. Making small talk with him over text messages is strange and unfamiliar.

WYATT: Everything's fine.

DAD: Good. I'm glad you're there. Have you considered your mother's request to come home in November?

And there it is. The real reason for his 'fatherly concern.' He's just looking out for my mom.

WYATT: I'm considering it. I'm just not sure what my plans are yet. I might actually take some time off after the opening.

DAD: That's fine, you've got more than enough time accrued. But it would mean a lot to your mother if you came home next month.

WYATT: I know, Dad. I just need to figure some things out.

My nondescript answer seems to satisfy him for now because the rest of the conversation goes back to the subject of work, the upcoming opening, and a problem we're having with our Victoria store.

We finish up our conversation, then as per usual, he ends without saying goodbye. I drop my phone on the couch and head to the shower, needing to wash off the sweat and the discontent. My hands come to rest on the wall as the hot water pelts down on my back. From this angle, the Valkyrie tattooed across my chest seems to almost stare back at me. My constant reminder of what I lost. As if I could ever forget.

My heart is heavy as I towel off. Pulling on a pair of sweatpants I go to the kitchen and straight to the liquor cabinet over the fridge. Grabbing a bottle of Japanese whiskey, I pour a healthy shot and toss it back, letting it burn down my throat. It might be a waste of good whiskey, but right now I don't care. I need the burn to drown out the rest of my pain. I pour another shot, even larger this time, and wander into the living room to sink down on the couch. I let my eyes drift out over the view of the backyard and the ocean view beyond. Unbidden, memories start to flood in.

The shed is still there, but it doesn't hold our bikes and skateboards anymore. The year we graduated from high school, my parents came and cleaned it all out, donating it to a local shelter. I haven't been back here in a couple of years, so I have no idea what's in there now.

The trampoline is gone now, but I remember I used to force Ryder to do backflip contests with me. He humoured me, even though I always won. Probably because most of the time I would go on and practice, while he would sit on the grass beside me, his nose buried in a book.

Which is why he was the one who was meant to be here right now, working for our family's company. He's the one who was meant to run the stores. He had the business sense, the passion for books, and the desire to carry on the legacy of Crawford Books.

Not me.

I never wanted this.

But because I left him with his last memory of being in a stupid fight with his twin brother, stepping into his shoes and fulfilling his life's ambition felt like the only decision I could make. He deserved that much from me, at the very least.

Fuck you, leukemia. Fuck you for taking my brother from me, for forcing me into a job, a life, I never wanted.

Fuck. You.

Chapter Four

Paige

"Good grief, their romance section is pathetically small. Yours is so much better."

"Mila, I appreciate your support, but please keep your voice down. I doubt the Crawford Books team want to hear disparaging remarks about their brand-new store." I grip the strap of my bag across my chest as my gaze darts around to see if anyone heard Mila's comment. She's not wrong, but still, the grand opening of a large store that has the potential to take away some of my business is not the time or place.

Mila simply shrugs. She likely has not made the connection between this store's opening and the potential impact on my store. While Dogwood Cove is half an hour away from Westport, it feels close enough that if I don't have a strong enough marketing plan, the opening of a large chain store such as Crawford Books could be my downfall. Truthfully, I didn't want to come to the opening today, out of a petulant desire to not be seen as supporting the competition in any way. But Mila needed to come to Westport to pick up some piece of equipment for her café and suggested we stop by and check it out.

It has been an eye-opening experience, to say the least.

"All I'm saying is, your store caters to a different audience. You've decorated with a personal touch, you carry a great variety of books, and you sure as hell ensure more diversity than what I'm seeing here." Mila gestures over to what I agree is a pathetically small romance section. Scanning the titles, I see very few authors of colour represented in the already slim selections available. Disappointing, really, when there are so many incredible authors out there, providing us with stories of love from their own voices.

Mila and I continue our walk-through of the store. I have to admit, they've set it up well, with space in the aisles, a few chairs scattered throughout, bright lighting, and enticing displays at the end of each shelf. We stop at a table laden with plated sandwiches and drinks. Mila picks up a scone and examines it critically before taking a small bite.

"Dry. Too dry," she comments before taking another bite. "Mine are way better. Hey, you could offer some scones and muffins in the store, if you want?"

I look at her in horror. "Food? Around my books? No, thank you. If people want to eat while they read, they can pay for the book first."

Mila laughs and rolls her eyes at me, but I know she means well. This isn't like it was with Wyatt; I've been around Mila long enough that I can read her social cues and know when she is teasing me.

The truth is, I have very particular opinions about books. When people eat, their fingers get greasy. And greasy fingers leave marks on pages. And that is unacceptable. It's up there with dog-earing the corner of a page instead of using a bookmark, or the ultimate faux pas — breaking the spine on a book.

Near the front of the store are an older couple who I recognize from the Crawford Books website. Hank and Giselle Crawford are the CEO and COO of Crawford Books. Along with Hank's brother, Paul, who acts as CFO, they took over the company from Hank and Paul's father, James, about ten years ago. As one of the largest bookstore chains in Canada, I made a point to research them before I opened my store. Their business model is solid and sustainable. There is no pattern of them eliminating smaller, independent stores on purpose, but the fact remains that they can provide a level of service and a volume of inventory that I can never hope to match.

I suppose it is unfair to call them my competition, as they are in another league. Yet, the pressure remains for me to ensure my store provides something this store cannot.

"Hey, isn't that the hottie from the café last week?"

Turning my head to follow Mila's direction, I feel a jolt of excited surprise to see Wyatt striding toward us. My mind flashes back to the two interactions we had last week at the store and then in the parking lot of the Dogwood Bluffs trail. Both times he was dressed quite casually, unlike today. His dark shirt is buttoned up to the top, tucked into some deep wine-coloured slacks. The sleeves are down, covering the tattoos I know he has on his wrist. Even his hair has been tamed and his face freshly shaven. Interesting. I wonder why he is dressed so formally for a bookstore opening. For that matter, why is he here at all? My curiosity is piqued.

"Paige, hey." His tone is low, and his eyes seem to dart around the room, only briefly landing on myself and Mila. If I were to guess, I would say he appears nervous. For what reason, I have no idea.

"Hello again, Wyatt," I reply, taking in the sudden flush of warmth across my skin. This time, my reaction doesn't catch me by surprise. After all, I had a similar response when I saw him at the trail. His sweaty shirt clinging to his muscles resulted in a sudden desire to touch him. I abstained, of course, but it was a new and not unwelcome thought. Now that I have finally acknowledged my attraction to Wyatt goes beyond that of mere appreciation for his appearance, I find myself enjoying these newfound experiences of desire.

Not that I plan on ever acting on them, of course. But it has been reassuring to finally feel a small sense of the lustful thoughts I read about in books and hear about from my dear friends.

"Wyatt? Hi. I'm Mila, we met briefly at my café last week. I'm one of Paige's best friends." Mila's interruption breaks my focus just in time for me to realize I had been staring at Wyatt for an uncomfortable amount of time. Any hope that he had not noticed is dashed when I see the small smirk on his face as his eyes dart my way, even while he shakes Mila's hand. Mortified, I drop my gaze down to the floor as Mila and Wyatt engage in conversation. It's so easy for her, and my envy creates a pulling sensation in my gut. I try not to dwell on my struggles with social interactions, after all, I've learned how to navigate my world — the town and my store — quite well, even incorporating new people into my circle, due to the intimate relationships my friends are in. But watching Mila converse with Wyatt so freely, seeing the animation on both of their faces as they discuss books, I find myself feeling jealous. I want that ease of conversation with him.

"Why are you here, Wyatt?" I blurt out, interrupting whatever they were talking about. They both turn to me, Mila with a curious expression on her face. She can obviously sense my discomfort right now. But Wyatt...he looks anxious at my question.

"Oh you know, I love books, so, when I heard this place was opening, I figured I'd stop by."

The words may make sense, but there's an artificial tone to his response. And I can't miss the way his gaze continues to survey the room, as if he is looking to see who might be listening. Thankfully, before my tendency toward blunt curiosity can force me into an even more awkward position of questioning him further, Wyatt shifts backward on his feet.

"Anyway, I better let you guys enjoy things. I'll, ah, see you around."

With a half-hearted wave in our direction, Wyatt turns and heads down an aisle toward the back of the store.

"He's hot, but kinda weird, am I right?"

"Yes."

Mila grabs my arm and turns me to face her. Surprise is written across her expression, and I frown, trying to determine what I have said wrong.

"Wait. Are you agreeing that he's hot, or that he's weird? Or both! Oh my God, did you just agree with me that you think Wyatt is hot?"

My eyebrows furrow in confusion. "Well, yes, he is, objectively speaking, an appealing man to look at."

"That's not what I mean, Paige. Your voice, when you said yes, it was all suggestive and breathy. The way you interrupted us. All of it. You *like* him."

"Nonsense. I don't even know him. How could I possibly like him?"

"Paige, I love you, but don't be obtuse. You know what I mean."

That's the problem, I do know exactly what she means. I simply don't feel ready to admit it.

"Mila, he is an attractive man. He is also a stranger. There's nothing more to it."

"I think there is, missy. And eventually you're going to have to spill the beans."

Later that week, I attend a yoga class at Serena's studio. This is rapidly becoming one of my favourite activities. Led by Summer, I find I greatly enjoy the meditative aspect of the practice. By tuning into my body and my breath, I am able to combine my favourite sensations from when I dance around the store after it is closed with the health benefits of the breathing techniques I have learned from my years of managing my asthma.

Normally, I also greatly enjoy spending the time with my friends. At least two or three of us try to attend each week, if not all of us. And after, we sometimes go to the apartment above Mila's café that is currently vacant and enjoy some tea together.

This week, however, I find myself not relaxing as I normally do. Because Mila and Serena will not stop talking about the Pleasure Party they have planned for our next book club meeting. Briefly I contemplate coming up with an excuse to miss the meeting, but somehow I know they won't let me get away with that. Not to mention, I truly enjoy our book club. Even if I do often have to keep the other ladies on task with actually discussing the book.

"Mae is super excited to join us. She agreed to read the book, and she's bringing a bunch of their new toy lineups for us. Oh, and she said she's got some prizes and giveaways, too." Mila carries over some mugs of tea and sets them down on the table, and Summer follows her with the rest. I pick mine up and blow on the steaming hot liquid, letting the fragrance of chamomile waft over me. Perhaps I can use the therapeutic benefits of aromatherapy to instil some calm in me to combat this agitation.

"I already told Paige, I'm buying her something to help her find her G-spot." Serena's voice sounds triumphant, and I turn a scowl in her direction.

"If I recall correctly, I told you not to waste your money."

Serena simply blinks owlishly at me. "And I told you, it wouldn't be a waste if it gets you in touch with your sexy side."

"I think she wants a certain hottie stranger to get in touch with her sexy side, not a toy..."

"Mila!" I bark out louder than I intended, but it works to get her attention, and she has the decency to look slightly contrite. Unfortunately, it's not enough to stop Summer and Ashley, the newest member of our group, from being curious.

"Who is she talking about, Paige?" Summer asks in her calm, soft voice. I enjoy Summer. She's quiet, and easy to be around. Her more relaxed energy fits with me easily. But right now, I am not pleased with her for asking that question.

"This seriously sexy dude who came into the café last week. I'm talking hot with a capital H. And then we saw him in Westport a couple days ago at that store opening we went to," Mila is quick to answer, earning another glare from me.

"It doesn't matter who he is. Wyatt isn't from here, therefore, he has probably already left town. And even if he hasn't, there was no indication in any of our interactions that he would be remotely interested in engaging in any sort of intimate activity with me." My voice is ridiculously high at the end, and my friends are all staring at me.

"Does he have shaggy hair and tattoos on his wrists?" Ashley asks. "Because a good-looking guy came by the winery yesterday for a tasting and bought a few bottles. I was visiting Finn and even I did a double take at this guy."

"Yes! Trees on his wrists, right, Paige?" Mila looks at me expectantly, waiting for me to confirm. Reluctantly, I incline my head in agreement.

"Hold on. You've seen a guy you're attracted to, twice, and you haven't told me about him?"

Even I can hear the hurt tone to Serena's words, and inwardly, I wince. And pointedly avoid correcting her that I have actually seen Wyatt more than twice. Not that I am counting...

"It was not an intentional oversight, I assure you. I simply didn't think my meeting Wyatt warranted a discussion, given the improbability of anything ever occurring between us." I touch Serena's knee, and she gives me a soft smile.

"But you thought about something happening with him, didn't you? You were attracted to him? That's a good thing, Paige."

I nod slowly. I cannot keep the truth from these women. They are my friends, they know me, all the parts of me, and for whatever reason, they accept me just the same.

"Yes, I was — am — attracted to Wyatt. He is a very...handsome man. And I did —" I pause, feeling the heat steal over my cheeks. I take off my glasses and wipe them on my shirt before putting them back on. "I did feel things that I hadn't felt before. I suppose they were the feelings of desire. But —" I hold up my hand because I can see Serena clamoring to interject "—nothing will ever happen. As I said, he is likely not even in town any longer, and even if he were, I have no intention of acting on my desires. I don't believe sexual relations are a worthwhile endeavour for myself."

Serena lets out a loud sigh, as if she is the one affronted by the conversation. "Paige, Paige, Paige. What are we going to do with you?" She lets her head fall to my shoulder, and I reach up and pat it somewhat awkwardly. It truly eludes me as to why my friends feel it is such an atrocity that I have no interest in sex. At least not in the same way they all seem to.

Although, secretly, I will admit, if there was ever someone I would consider exploring things with, it would be the mysterious Wyatt. Perhaps that is why it's a relief to me that he has likely left town by now. After all, I'm not even certain how to begin exploring an intimate relationship. And as much as I love these women, and as much as they already know about me and my lack of experience, I cannot bring myself to discuss this further with them. Not while things are so confusing and tumultuous in my own mind.

No, what I need is some time and space, from Wyatt and from the prying minds of my friends, to come to terms with my reactions to Wyatt. Time to process the new sensations and feelings, and file them away under interesting life experiences, and then move on from them.

Except that plan is obliterated when Ashley speaks.

"Paige, if Wyatt is the guy who came to the winery..." she bites her lip and lifts her shoulders almost apologetically. "He said he was going to be here for a few weeks, at least. He and Finn were talking about hiking trails."

Damn it.

Chapter Five

Wyatt

"Doesn't this remind you of the wine from that place, oh, what was it called? Ah yes, Prohibition Winery. We visited last time we were in California. Remember, Hank?"

My dad makes some random grunt of acknowledgment. He's been buried in emails for the past hour, despite Mom's numerous attempts to get us all to converse like some big happy family. Not that it'll work. It never really does, hasn't for years.

"Wyatt, have you had a chance to think about your plans now that the opening is over? We could use you in Victoria, or you could come back to the mainland for a while." Mom sounds so hopeful; I hate knowing that I'll be disappointing her, yet again. I close my eyes briefly and steel myself against the inevitable pain I know I'll see when I respond.

"Actually, I talked with Dad about taking some time off. Maybe a few weeks or so. We don't have any more openings coming up until spring, so I was hoping to get a break."

Sure enough, Mom is frowning. "But you'll try to come home for…November, right?"

She can't even bring herself to say the date. She never has. It's always just 'November,' never 'November 8th' or 'the anniversary of the day Ryder died.'

"I don't think so."

"Oh, Wyatt."

There it is. There's the pain, the disappointment, the grief. And here comes the tidal wave of guilt that always hits me, engulfing me, drowning me. Every fucking year.

"It would mean a lot to your mother if you would come home, son." Dad's voice chimes in, and I glance over to see him peering at me over the top of his computer screen.

"I know. I just can't. Maybe next year." My words sound hollow and land flat. I grab my glass of wine, a Meritage from a local winery my parents and I went to yesterday. It's good. But it still sticks in my throat as I take a long sip.

My guilt only builds as my mom walks over to the kitchen, busying herself with God only knows what. Dinner was catered, and the staff already cleared the dishes. There's nothing to do. When I see her hand lift to her cheek to swipe away what I imagine are tears, I feel my cold, broken heart crack even further. No matter how it may seem, I hate hurting my mom. I just know that trying to be with my parents on the anniversary of Ryder's death would hurt even more. More than I can handle.

"What's your plan, then? Take off and leave town, run away from everything?"

I pivot on my feet to face my father. "I'm not running away from anything."

He arches a thick eyebrow at me, challenging me.

"I'm not. I haven't taken a vacation in almost a year. Is it really a crime to want some time off?"

Dad lifts his hands up, but it comes across as placating, not surrendering, and it only serves to make me angrier.

"No one is saying you don't deserve to take a break, son. I'm just questioning why you can't take your vacation and maybe spend some time with your family, with the people who love you."

I snort in derision. The words want to fly off my lips that he doesn't love me, he loves to guilt me, but I hold back. After all, no one places more guilt on myself than I do.

"I'm not going anywhere right away," I say, forcing myself to speak more calmly, evenly. "I was hoping to stay here for a while, actually. Explore the area."

Mom comes over and sits down beside me, reaching a tentative hand over to touch my knee. "I think that's a lovely idea, honey. You and Ryder —" her voice cracks "— you both loved it here so much."

I lift my glass to my lips and drain it before standing up and walking over to grab the bottle. Without saying a word I top off my father's glass, earning a slight nod of thanks. The rest I tip into my glass. My parents leave for the mainland tomorrow, and I think I'll be making another trip to La Lune Rouge Winery to get some more wine.

As my parents start to talk about something that's going on back on the mainland, I let my mind drift. Unsurprisingly, my thoughts coalesce into an image of the woman who's been at the forefront of my mind for days now. A woman who intrigues me more than she should.

Suddenly, I'm struck with a vision of sitting on this couch, looking out the window at the view of the water. But it isn't my parents here with me, it's Paige.

Somehow, my parents managed to leave this morning without mentioning my coming home in November again. I'm sure that's not the end of it, but I'll take the small mercy, seeing as I'm ready to climb out of my skin right now.

As soon as their car pulls out of the driveway, I hurry upstairs and change into some lightweight clothes that I can climb in. Grabbing my gear and tossing it in the back of my car, I turn to the page I marked in the guidebook I bought from Paige that first day, and double-check the directions to where I plan to go.

The drive is short, and I keep the volume on the radio up high, letting some old-school Metallica fill the car and drown the noise in my head. When I cut the engine in the nearly empty parking lot at the base of the bluffs I plan on climbing, the silence is deafening. It's the same parking lot where I saw Paige after my hike, but I don't let myself dwell on that. I need the physical and mental burn of climbing, not the distraction of a woman right now.

Quickly, I get my rock climbing shoes on and grab my chalk bag and crash mat. Finding the boulder field, I nod hello to a couple of other climbers but find a spot by myself. My mind goes through the routine tasks of setting up to climb like it's second nature, which, in a way, it is. I may not have climbed in a month, but prior to that, it was a regular thing for me. Anywhere I traveled, I looked for places to climb. Whether it was indoor gyms or outdoor locations, I need the mental and physical challenge that rock climbing gives me. It calms me, quiets my mind, tires my body, and fills my soul.

When I reach the base of the first boulder I'm going to try, I take a few deep breaths. When my head is clear of thoughts of work, Ryder, and even Paige, I start to climb. The first route is fairly easy, and I hit the top hold quickly. Lowering myself down, I decide to try it again but challenge myself with finding only finger holds. That takes a little longer, and by the time I get back down, my heart is pounding and my arms are starting to ache. A few of the other climbers stop to say hi, and when I need a break, I join them with my protein bar and water. It's nice to just shoot the shit with people who don't give a fuck who I am or anything about me. We just talk climbing, local routes, and far away routes. I've been to Yosemite three times, and one other guy has as well, so we spend some time chatting about El Capitan.

Eventually, I hit the rock again. This time a new route, one that proves to be a lot more challenging than the others. I'm halfway up the boulder when it happens. Someone down on the ground laughs loudly, and it sounds so much like Ryder that my grip slips and my body slams into the rock. Wincing in pain, I manage to drop down to the ground cautiously before taking a look at my arm. A long gash is dripping blood. Fuck. That's probably going to need stitches.

Some other climbers help me wrap my sweater around my arm and pack up my gear. The entire drive to the hospital in Westport, I'm cursing and swearing at my stupidity for letting myself get distracted by a fucking laugh. The nurse at the triage desk winces when I walk in, and I look down to see the blood has soaked through the sweater wrapped around my arm. I grimace back at her as she hurries to sign me in and check my vitals before escorting me to a stretcher.

"I'll make sure a doctor comes over soon," she reassures me, then walks off quickly. I watch her go and see her stop by an older woman standing behind a desk, who I'm guessing is the doctor. They glance over at me, take in my bloody clothing, and the doctor's eyebrows raise up. I guess a small hospital like this doesn't get many bloody arms. Whatever. I'm tired, grumpy, sweaty, and in pain. I just want to get some fucking stitches and get out of here. I hate hospitals.

"Wyatt? I'm Doctor Grey, no relation to Meredith, I assure you." She gives me a wry grin that I don't return. Not in the mood for jokes right now. I grunt in acknowledgment, and she thankfully turns her attention to my arm. Carefully we unwrap the sweater, and she and the nurse clean it up. The gash ends up not being too long and only requires a few stitches. After Doctor Grey finishes up, she gives me a shot of antibiotics and instructions on the signs of infection to watch for, then at last, I'm free to leave.

As I walk out to the main lobby of the hospital, a familiar voice hits my ears.

"I'm here to see Doctor Sidhu for his respirology clinic."

I turn the corner to see Paige standing at a check-in desk. An unexpected wave of worry hits me out of nowhere. Paige is nobody to me. She's just a woman I am attracted to. Yet seeing her here, in a hospital setting, has me realizing that the attraction I feel may be more than just superficial. She intrigues me, she pulls me in, she makes me want to know her better.

But no amount of physical attraction is worth the risk of going through the pain of watching someone I care about endure sickness. And if she's here to see a respirologist, then she's someone I need to stay away from.

I won't go through that with anyone.

Never again.

CHAPTER SIX

Paige

I am irrationally angry.

I am angry at the delivery driver who dropped off four heavy boxes of books at the post office across the street from my store, simply because I had my *Back in Five Minutes* sign up and could not accept the delivery myself.

I am angry at my lungs for not responding as well to my controller inhalers as they usually do, prompting a visit to my respirologist's clinic at Westport General Hospital and an adjustment to my medications.

Most of all, I am angry at Wyatt. For distracting my mind each night as I try to sleep, causing me to turn fitfully and not get the restful sleep I need.

It is, without question, quite pointless to be angry at all of these things, as they are mostly beyond my control and therefore not worth wasting any emotional energy on. However, the fact remains that I have been in a foul, tired mood for the last two days and I am not certain how to move forward.

My foot lands in a puddle as I cross the street for the second time, carrying one of the boxes. "Damn it," I curse, shifting the heavy load in my arms and frowning down at the offending puddle.

"Let me take that."

Out of nowhere, the weight is lifted away from me. I look up to see the man who is the source of so much frustration, and my frown deepens. Wyatt gives me a curious glance but keeps walking toward my shop, forcing me to follow him. I open the door, and he sets the box down on the long counter beside the first one I managed to get here.

"Thank you," I say, somewhat begrudgingly. Wyatt dusts his hands off on dark jeans that are fitted to his strong legs in a far too appealing way.

"No problem." We stand there, looking at each other for a moment. "Well, I guess I'll get going," he says, and I nod mutely. He turns to go, and suddenly, I find my voice.

"Were you at the hospital in Westport two days ago?"

Wyatt freezes midstride. Slowly he turns back to me. "Yeah." Strange, his voice sounds hoarse.

"I..." I stumble over my words, filled with uncertainty. When I caught a glimpse of him hurrying away, I wanted to speak, to ask why he was there. But he was gone so quickly, and I had to see Doctor Sidhu. "I was there for an appointment; I thought I saw you," I finish lamely.

He says nothing, and not knowing how to handle the tense situation, I hurry to fill the silence. "I have asthma, and my respirologist holds a clinic there."

Wyatt's shoulders drop, as if he is releasing a deep breath. It almost seems that my explanation has brought him relief of some sort.

"Asthma. You just have asthma," he says, almost under his breath.

"Yes, since I was very young. For the most part, I have it under control, but occasionally, I have a flare up. Usually in relation to a virus or an environmental trigger."

He simply nods and the awkward feeling inside of me intensifies to the point of discomfort.

"Thank you for carrying that box," I say lamely as I pivot and take the few steps to the counter, picking up some papers there and shuffling them into a pile.

"Are there any more?" His voice comes from behind me, but closer, as if he has stepped toward me. When I peek over my shoulder at him, I see that he has, in fact, walked away from the door and over to where I'm standing.

"Any more..." I say, at a loss for what he's talking about. His close proximity is unnerving. I can see the shadow of facial hair across his jaw, a mole on his right cheek, and I smell a deep spicy scent that is as mysterious as he is.

"Boxes." His lips quirk up in a smile, the first one I've seen today, and I feel my lips turning up in response. I've never experienced my emotions to be so closely tied to someone else's. It's intriguing.

"Oh. Yes. Two more."

My mouth goes dry as Wyatt takes off his coat, then leans in close to me. So close. Just as my breath catches, with him inches away from me, he places his coat down on the counter behind me, and turns his head slightly. I can feel the warmth of his breath against my cheek.

"I'll go and get them for you," he rumbles softly, and then he's gone, taking his warmth and his spicy smell with him, and leaving me feeling far too flustered. I grab my inhaler out of my purse and take two puffs, because my breathing feels quite erratic. But deep down I know it isn't asthma causing that. It's Wyatt.

I busy myself with opening the boxes, checking for damaged books, and reviewing the packing order. Wyatt returns with one more box, then leaves immediately, I assume to get the last one. I don't enjoy needing assistance, but I am glad he stepped in. The boxes are heavy, there's no doubt.

This time when Wyatt comes back in the store, he sets the box down, and instead of leaving immediately as I assumed he would, he leans against the counter.

"What books did you order?" he asks conversationally.

I peer up at him from the floor where I've been stacking copies. "Most of these are the newest Jeffrey Morgan thriller. He's coming for a signing later this month."

He makes a sound of interest, and I say what I'm thinking without stopping to debate whether it is wise. "If you're still in town you should come."

He stares at me, those dark eyes burrowing into me, igniting something deep within. I feel goosebumps lift along my arms.

"Maybe I will."

All of a sudden, it's too much for me. The push and pull between us, the crackling tension that I am slowly coming to realize is perhaps not only one sided. I need a moment. I stand up swiftly and head to the door.

"I'm going next door to get some coffee. Do you want some?"

Wyatt nods, and I turn jerkily and open the door without even bothering to find out what he wants.

Outside, I take a moment to lean against the concrete pillar that divides my store from The Nutty Muffin bakery. I draw my breath in through my nose and out through my mouth, willing my heart to stop racing. But my efforts are in vain because the moment Mila sees me, her eyes widen and she comes rushing over.

"Are you okay? Why are you so flushed? Is it your lungs? Do we need to go back to the hospital?"

I manage to shake my head vigorously and spit out one word. "Wyatt."

She lets out a huff of laughter as her shoulders sag. "Oh, shit. You freaked me out, Paige! I thought you were having another attack or something, not getting all hot and bothered over a man."

My mouth opens to protest, to deny what she says is true, but I can't lie. "Mila, I don't know what to do," I answer honestly. "I look at him and I feel strange. I am preoccupied with thoughts of him, and when he is near, I feel warm all over. And I have this odd compulsion to touch him."

I feel vulnerable exposing myself to Mila like this, but she seems to take it in stride, wrapping her arms around me and giving me the hug I didn't realize I needed. The natural release of oxytocin from our embrace steadies me, and when I pull back, I feel calmer.

"Honey, you like him. You *want* him. I know this is new for you, but maybe just try to enjoy it. See where it goes," she says gently.

"I would like to do that, but what if —" I pause, licking my lips "— what if he rejects me when he finds out I have so little experience?"

"Oh, Paige," Mila murmurs.

"I have only been with two men, once each time. And that was less about desire and more about feeling it was a task necessary to move forward in my maturity."

Mila knows all of this, yet I can't stop myself from spilling it forth.

"I have never been drawn to a man the way I am with him and I don't even know his last name."

"Well, that's an easy thing to fix. Just ask him," she teases. "Next time you see him, just ask."

"He's waiting in my store right now," I mumble under my breath.

"What?" Mila exclaims, pushing my shoulder lightly. "You have a gorgeous man waiting for you and you're here talking to me?"

"I told him I was going to get coffee," comes my weak reply.

"So let's get you coffee and send you on your way."

We enter the bakery, and Mila hustles back behind the counter and busies herself making two drinks. Moments later, she passes them over the counter. "Latte for you and an Americano for him."

I look up in surprise. "Is that what he drinks?"

She gives me a wink. "Yep, and just think how amazed he'll be when you show up with it."

I smile gamely, but it must come out looking pained because Mila comes back around the counter and puts her arm around my shoulders, gently guiding me to the door. "Just be your usual amazing self, Paige. He's obviously interested, seeing how he's still around."

I consider that as she propels me out of the bakery, then stumble to a stop. "But..." my protest dies off.

Mila plants her hands on her hips and stares at me. "But nothing. You can do this. Just talk to him."

Just talk to him. But talking is when I know I come across as different. Awkward. Brainiac. Cold. Those are the words people have used to describe me in the past, and I don't want Wyatt thinking of me that way. Not that he's given me any indication that he thinks that of me, but still, I cannot deny that my nerves are high as I open the door to Pages.

At first glance, I don't see Wyatt, and my heart stutters at the thought that I took too long with Mila, and he may have left. Then I hear his voice from the side.

"Is this what women really want?"

He's leaning against the wall of what I call the *oxytocin stimulant* section, more commonly known as romance. The category name feels quite ironic, seeing as I have never personally experienced the alleged rush of oxytocin that is rumoured to accompany an orgasm.

Nonetheless, it's the largest section, and I was feeling proud of how I had carefully curated a selection that covered a vast array of tropes and subgenres, from authors of all different backgrounds and lifestyles. But now, seeing Wyatt standing there, what is normally my comforting escape seems like a trap. He lifts the book he's reading. It's a popular dark romance, with elements of bondage kink.

"Not all women, but some. Books like that one represent our deep and dark fantasies. The things that are not currently socially acceptable to enjoy in public but bring pleasure in private."

Wyatt puts the book back on the shelf and walks — no, stalks — over to me, taking the coffee cups from my hands and setting them on the shelf beside me. I inwardly wince at the idea of hot liquid next to my precious books, but there's no time to do anything about it because he's close to me again. Close enough that I can hear his intake of breath and smell his alluring scent again. My eyes flutter closed only to fly open when I feel the softest touch against my cheek.

"Your freckles..." he murmurs.

I turn away, but his hand cups my chin and tugs it back.

"They're incredible, Paige."

I'm speechless. No one has ever complimented my freckles before.

"Is that book what *you* secretly want?" His voice is ragged.

I drag my attention back to the conversation and away from the shocking compliment he just paid me. "No. Not me, personally."

Wyatt nods slowly, his eyes boring into me with a fiery intensity. "What do you want, Paige?"

"I...I don't know." I stumble over my words, but the truth is glaringly obvious. I want him. I just don't know what to do about it. Wyatt must sense my unease because he slowly takes a step back and picks up the forgotten coffee cups.

"Thanks for this." He takes a sip of the one marked with a W, and looks at me in surprise. "An Americano? How did you know?"

"I didn't. Mila did."

He chuckles quietly. "Well, now you do know."

"What's your last name?" I blurt out, "I know your coffee but not your last name."

His eyes shift down to the floor for a minute before meeting mine again. "James. Wyatt James."

I stick my hand out before I can stop myself, and he takes it with another chuckle.

"Sorry. I don't know why I did that," I say lamely.

"It's all good. Do I get to know your last name?"

"Millstone."

Wyatt gently squeezes my hand before letting go. "Well, Paige Millstone, this has been nice. But I should probably let you get back to work."

"Right. Work. Yes, I should." I turn around, suddenly at a loss as to what I need to do when all I can think about is feeling Wyatt's hand in mine again. I spy the boxes still stacked on the counter. "I should finish unpacking that."

I hurry over and start pulling books out, alternating between wanting him to come closer and wanting him to leave.

He makes the decision for me, and a moment later I hear the bell over the door jingle.

"I'll see you soon, Paige."

It's only when I hear the door close behind him that I let out the breath I didn't realize I was holding.

That night, I cannot fall asleep. I try meditating, but lose focus too many times. A warm cup of chamomile tea does nothing. Neither does a shower. As I flip my pillow over for the third time, my legs squeeze together in an attempt to ease the strange ache that I feel. I've felt it before, but typically only when reading one of the historical romance novels I greatly enjoy. It's a pleasant ache, when it isn't keeping me up at night. But I haven't read anything this evening.

In the past I've simply ignored the sensation. It has never led to anything satisfactory; both times I engaged in intercourse were rather perfunctory. Why I think this should be any different, I don't know, but Serena's comments when we were discussing the upcoming sex toy party come back to mind. *A woman's sexual pleasure is a thing to celebrate.*

My hand trails down to the waistband of my pajama pants. I slide under the elastic, and the first touch of my finger against my clitoris has my hips lifting. *That is different.* I experiment with different motions, fast and slow, soft touches and more firm ones. Nothing quite feels right, and nothing seems to further the sensations beyond that initial spark. I still ache, and now my frustration is mounting. I continue, determined to figure out why my friends feel so inclined to encourage me in finding my way to sexual pleasure. After several minutes, nothing has changed. I let my head fall back on my pillow and close my eyes.

A picture of Wyatt fills my head. The way his breath felt against my cheek. The warmth that emanates from him. A vision of his hand replacing mine has my fingers moving again, this time sliding in and out of my noticeably damp folds. This is new. Exciting. Perhaps I'm on the right path now. I keep the image of Wyatt firmly in place as I speed up my movements. Something is building, and I try not to get too eager, lest it disappear. The intensity grows. My breath speeds up, and I almost stop for fear of triggering my asthma, but I resolutely push on.

"Yes!" I gasp when I feel my body begin to spasm, but then it's over. I think. One small spasm, a mild sense of warmth, and now nothing. If anything, it's uncomfortable to still be touching myself at this point, so I stop, pulling my hand free and letting out a frustrated groan.

Once again, my body has proven to me that I am simply not a sexual being.

Yet, as I lay in bed, trying to sleep after washing my hands, I can't help but wonder one important thing.

Would it be different with Wyatt?

Chapter Seven

Wyatt

Taking some time off was a good idea. The freedom to wake up each day whenever I want, and spend my time outside, away from suits and computers and meetings has given me a much needed reset to my energy. But when night falls and it gets too dark to safely be out in the forest, I'm faced with an empty house. At least in the city I have people I can go out with, there's always a willing woman ready to come home with me if we're in the mood, or there's work to catch up on. Here, there's none of that. And I'm starting to go a little stir-crazy. Which is why tonight, I decided not to spend another evening at home alone, and instead, I head to the pub I noticed on one of my drives around town.

Hastings is pretty full when I walk inside. I guess this is where everyone goes when it's time to get out for an evening. I make my way to the bar and signal to the guy serving drinks down at the other end. He gives a nod of acknowledgment, and I settle in to wait. Looking out over the room, I don't realize I'm looking for Paige until my eyes land on her. She's sitting at a table with several other people, including the woman I now recognize is Mila.

I came close to kissing Paige yesterday. When I saw her carrying those boxes, I couldn't have stayed away, even if I tried. I was raised to always offer help to someone who appeared in need. And when she told me why she was at the hospital, the relief I felt was surprising. Not that asthma isn't a big deal, I know it is. But I also know it's easily managed. It's not the death sentence that Ryder's cancer was.

And yes, that's a relief, but it's also a complication. Because it makes it that much harder for me to come up with a reason to resist my attraction to Paige. Granted, I'm almost certain that even if she was open to starting something with me, it would be for something a lot more committed than I'm willing to do.

"What can I get you?"

A deep voice has me turning around to see the bearded bartender looking at me with open curiosity.

"Whatever Saison you have on tap would be great," I reply. He gets to pouring and minutes later a frosty glass is slid across the counter to me.

"You're new here, aren't you?"

I put the glass down after taking a sip. Apparently he's a chatty bartender. "Yeah. Not staying long, just a few weeks."

His head moves up and down slowly. "Well, you found the best beer selection in town and some wicked burgers. Name's Dean." His hand is out and I reach over and shake it firmly.

"Wyatt."

His eyes widen in recognition, which has me confused for a moment.

"I've heard about you. My wife Riley is friends with the other ladies, and they gossip more than a group of teenagers. I've heard your name come up a couple times."

"Good things, I hope," I remark casually, even though on the inside, I'm sweating. What if one of them has figured out who I really am and tells Paige. Unbidden, my eyes dart back over to her.

"They're all taken except Paige and Serena, so careful with who you're looking at."

There's a warning edge to Dean's voice, and I look back quickly. "Don't worry. I'm not here to cause any problems." He takes my reassurance with another silent nod. "Actually, I am curious about Paige."

At the obvious narrowing of his gaze, I hurry to continue. "She's interesting, that's all."

"Paige is a fucking gem. And anyone who messes with her, messes with all of us."

Jesus Christ, what is this, the small-town mafia? I've dug myself a hole without even realizing it when two men come up on either side of me.

"Dean, my man, can we get another pitcher of Route 49?" The bigger guy wearing a plaid shirt speaks before turning to me. "Hi. I'm Ethan."

"This is Wyatt. He was asking about Paige."

There's a meaningful manner behind Dean's words that I don't have time to unpack before Ethan folds his thick arms across his chest and fixes me with a stare.

"Really. You're Wyatt."

I stand up straight. No lumberjack wannabe is going to make me feel intimidated. "I've met her a few times and I think she's a cool lady. That's all."

"She is. She's awesome."

My head shakes back and forth before I can think of the intelligence behind the move. "Look, guys, I don't know what's given you the idea I'm some asshole here to prey on your women, but I'm not. I'm only in town for a little while, and I came out tonight to have a drink, maybe hang out a bit."

"Wyatt? Are these men bothering you? Their body posture seems quite defensive."

I spin around at Paige's voice. "Hey, nah, it's okay. Just guys talking."

Ethan shifts subtly so he's almost in front of me. "Just asking some questions, Paige."

Man, if looks could kill. I hide my smile as I watch Paige put her hands on her hips and fix Ethan with a glare that lowers the temperature of the room several degrees. "Ethan Monroe, you may be mayor of this town, but you are not in charge of me, or anyone with whom I choose to spend my time. It's obvious to all of us —" she gestures to the women at the table behind her "— that you, Reid, and Dean are interrogating Wyatt for no reason."

Finally, she looks at me, and even in the dim light, I can see the faint blush come across her cheeks. I give her a reassuring smile, wanting desperately to reach out and tuck the strand of hair that has come loose from her bun behind her cheek.

"Wyatt has been a customer at Pages. That's all."

Damn. Her immediate minimizing of our interactions stings. But it also serves the purpose of getting the guys off my back because I see Ethan's posture soften. Deciding to be the bigger man, I put my hand out toward him. "Wyatt. Nice to meet you, Ethan." After a second, he unfolds his arms and takes my hand, shaking it firmly. I turn to the other guy, who has a friendly grin and isn't nearly as big as Ethan.

"Reid. Nice to meet ya, Wyatt." I return his easy smile, then turn my attention to the person I really want to talk to.

"Hi, Paige."

She gives the men on either side of me one more fixed look, and again, I'm fighting back a chuckle at how they turn and leave.

"Nicely done," I comment, taking a sip of my beer, trying to project a relaxed energy, even though I'm weirdly excited she's here.

"They mean well," she says as she leans her elbows on the bar next to me.

"Friends are a good thing."

"They are, indeed. I am lucky to have people like them who care about me."

Damn it, we're back to the stilted, awkward conversation. That's not what I want. But now isn't the time to think about what I really want.

"Read any good books lately?" I ask casually, before taking it to the next level. "Maybe another romance or two? What do they call them...bodice rippers?"

Clearly, the key to unlocking Paige is literature. Her body visibly relaxes, and her bow shaped lips curve up into a small smile.

"Bodice rippers refer to historical romance. This month my focus is on mafia romance, as that is the theme of our book club discussion."

Her answer makes me cough on my beer, but I recover quickly. "Mafia, huh? Not gonna lie, Paige, the way your friends were crowding me earlier felt a little bit like some thugs coming for a beatdown. Is Dogwood Cove a secret hub for an underground crime syndicate?"

I'll be damned if Paige's laughter isn't the cutest damn thing I've ever heard.

"Hardly. Although, I feel I must apologize once more for their behaviour." Her hand tentatively reaches out and rests on my arm. "They mean well, but that was out of line."

Cautiously, I lift my own hand and lay it over hers. I feel her fingers jump, then settle against my arm again. She's staring down at where we're connected.

"Paige, it's fine. I respect the hell out of any guy who will defend a woman. Even if it isn't necessary. I'm not the big bad wolf, after all." I wink and earn myself another laugh. Fuck, I'll do whatever it takes to make her laugh.

"Would you like to come and join my friends and I for a drink?"

Well, shit. Of course I want to, but if I stand up right now, I'll have to do some careful positioning to hide how affected I am by nothing more than her beauty and her laugh. Paige hops off her stool, and I stand up behind her, shifting my legs slightly. Fuck, she makes me feel like a horny teenager all over again.

Paige leads me over to the table and makes quick introductions. On the other side of Mila is Jackson, who introduces himself as the town vet. He seems nice enough. Next to Mila is Serena, who gives me a mischievous smile that I don't have time to think about as Paige continues introductions. Down the table is a guy I recognize from the day my parents and I went to the local winery. He says his name is Finn, and the blonde beside him is his fiancée, Ashley. Then Reid and Ethan, the two guys who came up to the bar, and their significant others, Abby and Summer.

"Summer is the one who runs the resort I told you about," Paige prompts, gesturing to the woman next to Ethan, who of course, has an arm stretched over her shoulder and is still looking at me with a healthy amount of suspicion.

"Right. It would be great to chat sometime, Summer. I'm ah, interested in possibly starting an outdoor venture tour company in the area," I say, hating how easily the lie rolls off my tongue.

Summer opens her mouth to respond, but Ethan beats her to it. "As the town mayor, you'll have to also meet with me for permitting enquiries."

Summer elbows him before giving me a warm smile. "Easy there, lumberjack." That makes me snort, given how I thought of him when I first saw the guy. "Wyatt, I would love to chat about your plan. We could use someone experienced and knowledgeable to guide visitors in the area. I get plenty of questions about hiking trails, kayaking, rock climbing — all kinds of stuff I just can't answer."

Well, shit. That actually surprises the crap out of me. Even though it's always been my true dream, what I've actually wanted to do with my life, the idea that it could actually be a real possibility never occurred to me. But as quick as that flash of hopeful excitement hits me, it's dashed by a wave of guilt. I can't leave my parents and Crawford Books. I can't disappoint them like that, they need me.

"Yeah, that would be great," I reply to Summer, the words sounding hollow to my ears. Summer settles back in her chair, seemingly satisfied with my response.

Paige leads us to two empty chairs at the end of the table and we sit down. She's quickly drawn into conversation with Ashley, who's on her other side, so I take a minute to just look around and take in everything.

Aside from Jacob, I don't exactly have a lot of close friends. You could say I'm too busy with work, but the truth is, people look at me differently when they realize I'm Wyatt Crawford, of *that* Crawford family. Our net worth is well-known, and even though I've always tried to avoid the spotlight and shied away from media attention, I'm not exactly unknown. That's why it's been such a welcome surprise that no one here seems to know, or at least, if they do know, they don't care about who I am. Do I feel bad giving Paige a slightly inaccurate name? Yeah, I do. But it's not a lie. My name really is Wyatt James, I just left off my last name.

Eventually, I'm pulled into conversation with Finn, who turns out to be interested in rock climbing. He admits he's more of an indoor gym guy, but we make plans to go over to Westport where there's a place we can check out. The rest of the evening passes, and before I know it, we've all had too many beers to drive home. Dean assures all of us we can leave our cars in the parking lot, so as a group we head out.

Plans are made for who's walking and who's getting a ride. When I hear Paige protesting that she's fine to walk, I seize the chance. "I'll walk you home," I say, leaving no room for argument. Mila, who was apparently trying to get Paige to call a cab, gives me an enigmatic smile.

"Perfect. Thank you, Wyatt." She turns to Paige. "Text me when you get home, and I'll see you tomorrow for breakfast."

The women embrace, and I stand back as the group scatters in different directions. Finally, it's just Paige and me. "I do not require an escort, Wyatt, you're welcome to make your own way home regardless of how Mila may have made it sound." Paige is looking at the ground, her hands twisting nervously in front of her.

Impulsively, I reach out and take her hand in mine. "Maybe I need an escort, did you ever think of that? I'm not from here, Paige, I might get lost." I give her a smile to reinforce my teasing, and it does the trick.

"I highly doubt that. You seem quite familiar with our town."

We start off walking, heading toward the residential neighborhood where my family's house is. "Are you this way?" I ask, wanting to make sure she isn't taking me seriously. Make no mistake, I have every intention of walking her safely home. She nods and we make our way down the quiet sidewalk. "I used to come here with my family. My parents still own the house, that's where I'm staying." I try to not give away too much that would indicate my family's wealth.

She's still holding my hand, but loosely, so I experiment with tightening my hold. After a brief moment, she surprises the hell out of me by taking the lead and threading our fingers together. Her eyes dart up to me, seeking reassurance, and I squeeze gently. We walk in an easy silence. This feels so natural, so comfortable. Which, I have to admit, is not what I expected. I figured Paige would put up way more walls and defenses. Not that she's letting me in, but I'll take this small victory. Every moment spent with her only makes me want more. She's so different from any woman — hell, any person — I've ever known. So free of pretense, content in herself. There's a vulnerability to her, but also strength. It makes me want to just enjoy whatever time and attention she'll give me.

"This is my place." We come to a stop outside a small, cute-looking house. I gently tug on her hand until Paige is facing me.

"I had fun tonight. Your friends are great."

Her lower lip is tugged between her teeth, and fuck, do I want to pull it free.

"Yes. They are exceptional individuals."

I smile at her description. Only Paige would call her friends exceptional individuals. Deciding on impulse to take a risk, I lean forward, taking in the widening of her eyes. I lightly press my lips to her forehead, and I'm close enough to hear the tiny gasp she makes when we connect.

"Good night, Paige."

Chapter Eight

Paige

The amount of time I have spent dissecting and analyzing the implications behind Wyatt's lips touching my forehead is astronomical, and entirely illogical. Yet, I cannot seem to stop. In twenty-four hours, I have relived that moment no less than thirty-three times. Possibly more, seeing as I only started counting after the third or fourth occurrence.

Without a doubt, this is a terrible time to be as distracted as I am. I nearly spilled a glass of water all over some books this morning, and not just any books. Jeffrey Morgan's books. His signing event is tomorrow. He is not the first author I have hosted at Pages, but he is one of the most successful and well-known. He is also proving to be the most challenging.

His agent had sent a list of requirements earlier in the week. Distilled water, room temperature, in a glass cup — not plastic. Five black gel ink pens, to be lined up to the right of the books he will be signing. No more than six books in a stack at any given time. Visits with readers to be limited to two minutes, maximum.

Nothing entirely unreasonable, per se, just a lot to manage on my own, and rather persnickety. Not for the first time, I find myself wishing I had the financial resources to hire a staff member on a regular part-time basis. Someday. But not today.

Today I am quite simply flustered from rushing with final preparations. Jeffrey and his agent are coming by this evening to ensure I have everything set up according to their specifications, so I decided to close the store early so I could clean and organize the shelves adequately, and triple-check my display of Jeffrey's books.

Just as I'm shifting a stack of books from a lower shelf up to an end cap, the bell over my door jingles.

"We're closed, my apologies, I should have placed a sign up," I call out. A sensation I can truly only describe as a vibration of awareness runs up my spine seconds before I hear his voice.

"I came by to see if you need any help. I was getting some coffee next door and Mila mentioned you were busy getting ready for tomorrow."

I straighten and slowly pivot on my foot to see Wyatt standing by the door, his hands in the pockets of dark jeans. My traitorous heart starts to speed up, but I am starting to become accustomed to my reaction at his presence. Now that I have identified and acknowledged it as sexual attraction, it no longer confuses me. Does it still overwhelm me? Yes. Do I have any clue how I wish to proceed? No.

"Thank you for the offer, but as you can see, I am almost finished."

His eyes take in the display and the signing table I have positioned near the back of the store to allow for a lineup.

"You need to move the table to a more central location to increase visibility."

"I have always held signings near the back to allow more space for the line to form."

"But if the lineup has to go outside, that will make it seem more enticing to people on the street. More visibility."

I consider what he has said. If I were to move the table, it would allow for better flow to the checkout counter, which would be preferrable. Decision made, I walk over to the table and begin moving items off of it to facilitate the relocation. Unbidden, Wyatt walks over and joins me, and we work in a companionable silence until the table is positioned centrally in the store. As I set Mr. Morgan's requested items on the table, Wyatt starts to arrange the books to be signed in perfectly aligned stacks of six.

"You have good instincts about this," I comment, and out of the corner of my eye, I am certain I see him flinch. An odd reaction to a compliment. But his response quickly dispels any curiosity.

"I've taken some courses in marketing."

"Where did you attend university?"

Wyatt puts down the last stack of books, then leans his hips against the table and I watch out of the corner of my eye, trying not to be obvious in my admiration of the way his arms strain against the fabric of his shirt when he crosses them over his chest.

"Why do you ask so many questions?"

His casual tone is at odds with the sharp words. I will not let him see that I am ruffled. "I have a curious mind."

"Yeah, I got that, I'm just wondering why. What made Paige Millstone so curious?"

I slowly spin around to face him, adopting a similar posture against the shelf next to me. Wyatt's voice is open, and free of judgment. He seems to genuinely want to know more about me, making me feel slightly guilty for my initial reaction of self-defence.

"My parents chose to homeschool me, which had the natural consequence of limiting my interactions with my peers. There were many reasons, but the primary one was that when I was young, my asthma was not well controlled. I was missing so many days of school, they chose to pull me and teach me from home. Unfortunately, the lack of social engagement led me to be quite inquisitive about, well, everything. Since I couldn't go places and learn myself, I asked questions."

I continue to study his face as openly as he does mine and am filled with relief that there still seems to be no judgment. I suppose a therapist would have their work cut out for them trying to unpack why I am so concerned with this man judging me, when all signs point to him being a temporary fixture in my life.

"I have to admit, I was wrong about you."

His comment takes me by surprise, and my hands clench at my sides, waiting for him to continue.

"When I met you, I figured you were shy, quiet." He shrugs, and dare I say, he looks embarrassed. "I was wrong. You're something else, Paige."

I am burning with a desire to ask him exactly what he means by that, but as I open my mouth to speak, the door to the store opens again. Both Wyatt and I startle at the intrusion.

"Miss Millstone?"

The nasally voice makes my skin crawl in an unpleasant way as I take in the two men standing in the doorway. One of them has what is undeniably an air of arrogance, examining my store as you would the bottom of your shoe if you were looking for excrement. I recognize Jeffrey Morgan from his book cover, and given the unending list of demands and changes from his agent, I am unsurprised that this is my first impression of him. The other, who I deduce is the man who spoke, must be his agent Michael Lazlo, or Mick, as he told me to call him. He's the one who approaches, first looking to Wyatt with a very curious expression on his face. It almost seems as if he recognizes him, but Wyatt turns away and my attention is pulled by Mick.

"I see you moved the signing table from where you indicated it would be in our last conversation."

Criticism drips from his tone, and Wyatt's shoulders tense.

"I, we, felt it would allow for an improved flow throughout the store as well as generate more interest with a longer line outside. The weather is promising to be mild tomorrow, so there should be no concern about customers waiting outside."

"Mick, the lighting in here is horrendous. We'll have to refuse any selfies. Do we have a photographer coming Miss Miller?"

"It's Millstone," I correct Jeffrey Morgan, who has finally made his way to where Mick, Wyatt, and I are standing.

"Right. Fine. Photographer?"

"No, I did not. Mick did not indicate one would be necessary," I reply firmly.

Jeffrey sniffs derisively. "Then there will be no photographs."

"But your fans," I sputter, and he interrupts me with a wave of his hand.

"*My* fans would never dream of accepting a less than flawless product. That includes photographs. If you hope to ever have an author of my calibre grace your store with their presence in the future, Miss Miller, I suggest you think of something as basic as a photographer."

I am left utterly speechless. Not only has he paid no attention to my correction on my last name, but to have been spoken to in such a condescending way is a new experience for me, and not one I care to ever repeat. Rubbing salt into the wound, Jeffrey Morgan turns his back to me, facing Wyatt and Mick.

"Have we met?" he asks Wyatt, and I'm slightly mollified to still hear an extremely condescending tone to his voice. At least he isn't a misogynist, just wildly disrespectful and arrogant.

"No."

Wyatt's abrupt dismissal of both Jeffrey and Mick goes even further to soothe my injured pride.

"Humph."

Jeffrey pivots away from Wyatt and returns to the table we set up for him. Never have I met someone with such exacting demands and such a complete disregard for basic manners and respect. How this man has amassed such a legion of dedicated fans is beyond me, but the number of pre-orders I received for his book was the highest I had ever acquired for any book. Obviously, they've never met him in real life.

"These stacks are too tall." Jeffrey's pompous voice rings out and my eyes flutter closed momentarily. I am not often one to use common colloquialisms, but I do believe the phrase *is this guy for real* is appropriate in this moment.

"The instructions I was given were stacks of six." I pride myself on how calm I manage to modulate my voice.

"No *more* than six. Appropriate ergonomics are important, and if the stack is too high or too low, the angle can be damaging to my wrist. This book is thicker than my previous works, therefore, six is too high. One could construe your choice as a breach of contract, Miss Miller."

My mouth falls open in shock. But before I can start to formulate a response, Wyatt's voice penetrates my shock.

"Paige, do you have a copy of the contract you signed with Mr. Morgan easily available?"

The cold, firm tone of his voice startles me. In our brief interactions, I have never heard him sound this way. I nod, and quickly go to my back office to find the document. My eyes scan it as I walk back, although to be frank, I'm uncertain what I should look for. When I reach Wyatt, the look he gives me speaks volumes. *Will you let me help you?* is the message I receive, and when I hand him the contract, I'm graced with a warm smile full of appreciation and respect. Then Wyatt's focus turns to the document. A moment later, that firm, in control voice is back.

"Mr. Morgan, as you can see, your agent signed this contract with Miss Millstone. Nowhere does it state a height specification for the stack, a request for a photographer, or requirements for positioning of the table. The expectations that *are* laid out here go well above and beyond any reasonable requests of a bookstore owner. You are the product in this situation, Mr. Morgan, and a product is replaceable. You would do well to remember the stores that invite you for signings are doing *you* a favour with all of their marketing efforts. Not the other way around."

The silence when Wyatt stops speaking is deafening. But the thundering of my heart feels so loud, I cannot comprehend how they aren't all hearing it. Having him stand up for me and my store like that is awakening in me the part of my heart I have kept hidden. The part that longs for a partner in life. Someone to stand by my side and walk with me so I'm not alone. I had accepted years ago that this was not ever going to happen. That good friends and my parents were the only connections I would ever have.

But Wyatt James is unraveling that belief with everything he says and does.

He's bringing to life parts of my being that I thought didn't exist.

He's making me want things I never imagined wanting.

Arousal. Passion. Love.

Just as the second wave of a tsunami is often more forceful than the first, the second wave of realization hits me harder.

Wyatt may be awakening many dormant aspects of my heart and my personality, but he won't be around long enough to do anything about that. Not to mention, aside from the kiss to my forehead last night, I have no verifiable evidence that he would be open to engaging in some sort of an intimate relationship with me.

For all I know, the flirtatious nature he sometimes displays in my presence is par for the course for him. I am unlikely to be anything special, regardless of what he said when he left me last night.

Then again, I have no way of determining his thoughts or intentions without outright asking, or simply acting on my own thoughts and desires. That is a thought-provoking observation, but not one I can act on at this present moment. Right now, my priority must be on the situation in front of me. Raising my hands in a placating gesture, I look from one pompous ass to the other.

"Mr. Morgan, Mick, I assure you that I feel confident tomorrow will be a success. I have, as you can see from the contract, done everything that was requested of me. Now if we are done here, I would like to finish cleaning, so that I can go home for the evening. We'll reconvene tomorrow for the signing."

I can see out of the corner of my eye that Wyatt's face is filled with what I can only describe as admiration when I finish talking. Mick obviously has some modicum of decency given the chastised expression he bears; Jeffrey Morgan is a lost cause, I suspect, as he continues to look around the store with contempt.

Thankfully, they take my pointed suggestion and leave.

"Thank you for your support with them. I must admit, I am glad you were here."

At my words, Wyatt stalks over to me, stealing the air from my lungs with surprise when his large hands cup my face. My pulse starts to quicken, thinking he may kiss me. But he doesn't, much to my disappointment.

"They were out of fucking line. No one should ever have to tolerate the disrespectful way they were speaking to you. Make no mistake, you handled them perfectly well, and even if I wasn't here, I have no doubt you would've managed. But I couldn't stand by and let them verbally assault you like that. You deserve respect. And so much more."

His thumbs gently stroke my cheek, eliciting a small shiver down my spine. His eyes grow heavy, lowering halfway closed. I lean in, slowly, cautiously, until my head turns and rests against his chest. It isn't the contact I truly crave, but it feels deliciously sensual for me, all the same. His hands trail down my back, coming to rest in the curve of my lower spine.

"Paige..." my name rumbles out from his chest, echoing through my ear.

I want to be bold. I want to leave my comfortable, easy existence. I want to step off the edge, into the unknown of lust and desire.

So I do.

Lifting my head off his chest, I tilt my gaze up. Slowly, one hand travels up his arm, some part of my mind cataloguing the muscles I feel bunched and tense under the fabric of his shirt. As it always is around him, my ability to focus on multiple things at once disappears, and all I am aware of is him. His scent, the sound of his breathing, the tightening of his hands on my hips.

I reach the longer hair at the nape of his neck and slide my fingers through the soft strands. His mouth opens slightly. Anticipation has already begun to spark throughout my body. When I lift up onto my toes and close the inches that separate us, that trickle of pleasure turns into a cascading free fall.

His lips are soft.

Why this surprises me, I don't know. Perhaps my lack of experience with these types of activities has predisposed me to expect men's mouths to be rougher.

Hesitantly, I move my mouth against his, waiting for him to respond. Mere seconds pass before I feel him give in to the inevitability of our kiss with a low groan. His body melts into mine but the pressure is balanced by his hands spreading across my back, holding me in place.

Had I known kisses were capable of igniting a fire within me that is burning as strong as I am right now, I may have indulged in this more often. However, I suspect it would never be as good as it is with Wyatt. Why? I have no idea. And that confounds me.

His tongue licks along the seam of my mouth, and although I have never kissed a man this way, I open to him readily. We meld together effortlessly. Our tongues tangle, darting in and out, teasing and tantalizing. This is a first kiss that should be written about in every romance book everywhere. Wyatt moves a hand down to cup one globe of my bum as the other continues to hold my body to his. When he squeezes gently, the corresponding rumbling sound he makes sounds deliciously out of control. And when he presses his hips into mine lightly, I pull back with a start.

"Is that..."

The corner of his lip lifts up, but ever the gentleman, Wyatt doesn't force me back into his arms. "Yeah. Sorry. I can't seem to help it around you, Paige. You're just so —"

I cut him off with the press of my lips to his once again as the realization hits me.

I'm doing this to him. Me. Paige Millstone, who has never experienced an orgasm, is causing Wyatt James to feel aroused. And judging by the significant bulge he pressed against me, I believe it is safe to say Wyatt is at least as interested in seeing where this goes as I am.

If not more so.

The question is, what now?

CHAPTER NINE

Wyatt

I stayed away from the bookstore yesterday. I sure as fuck didn't want to; the very thought of Jeffrey Dickhead Morgan treating Paige like garbage had me at a level ten of rage in an instant. But I've met him before. Years ago, at an event Crawford Books sponsored. And he came dangerously close to recognizing me, I could tell by the way he looked at me.

My conscience tells me I should tell Paige the truth about who I am. I wanted to, I still do. And I don't really know why I don't, except that it's nice to not feel beholden to the expectations that come with being a Crawford.

And then she kissed me. Correction, she kissed Wyatt James. That distinction is not lost on me.

Instead of going to the signing, I found a grueling six-hour hike in Strathcona Provincial Park and shut off my phone. By the time I got back to town, the signing was over, and I drove straight home and did my best not to picture Paige as I jerked off in the shower.

Spoiler alert, I failed. And it was her name I shouted out when I painted the shower wall with my release.

Her confident handling of Mick and Jeffrey yesterday was such a goddamn turn on. And the way she did it with her dignified words revealed her backbone of steel. She might claim to struggle with social interaction, but I don't see it that way. I see an elegant, composed woman who isn't afraid to let her intelligence show. She takes no bullshit and gives no bullshit.

She's tempting. Too tempting. Because for all her inner strength, she's also fragile. Vulnerable. After I got home from the bookstore the night before the signing, after we kissed and I felt her body pressed up against mine, my mind went down a dark path. Call it dramatic, call it overreacting, I don't care; I can't handle having someone else in my life who's sick. And memories of seeing her at the hospital refuse to leave me alone. Even though asthma is a controllable disease, her delicate body could fail her at any time. And I don't think I would survive someone else I care about leaving me. Which is another reason why I needed to keep my distance yesterday. Because I won't be able to stop at just a kiss the next time.

But fuck, what a kiss it was. Her enthusiasm surprised me. I can't figure out if she's a virgin, or inexperienced, or if it's simply her way of interacting, but something about her screams innocence. Which made the passion of our kiss all that more intense.

I can't avoid her forever, I know this. Which is part of the motivation behind my going to Camille's, the café next to The

Nutty Muffin. I've tried their soup before and was impressed. Mila is more than just a competent baker. She clearly knows her way around a kitchen, and around running a successful business.

Once I've placed my order for a grilled panini and soup, I take a seat and open the news app on my phone. I'm thumbing through the headlines when I hear a soft voice say my name. I look up to see Summer smiling down at me.

"Hi, Summer," I reply, glancing behind her to see if her hulking fiancée is with her. He isn't, and when I look back at her, she's smirking at me. Damn.

"Ethan's at work. He won't harass you again, trust me, I gave him shit for what he pulled at Hastings the other night. He just feels the need to protect everyone. I'm sorry you got caught up in that."

"It's fine. I respect that he's watching out for Paige."

"Anyway, I was hoping to see you again." Summer pulls out the chair opposite me and sits down. "I've been thinking a lot about your business plan. Up for a little shoptalk over lunch?"

I shrug my shoulders because what else can I do. It's not like I can tell her that the entire idea is a pipe dream, a fantasy I dreamt up with my dead brother years ago.

"Here's the thing. The resort has only been open just over a year, but every weekend I get people asking for my advice on hiking trails, where they can rent kayaks, where they could go on a trail ride, or fishing, or any number of things that I don't have answers for. If you're interested, I would love to discuss how we could work together. I've got some space in the main building of the resort you could use as an office, and maybe in return my guests could get a small discount? I wrote down a list of everything I could remember being asked about over the last year."

She slides a piece of paper across to me, and I glance at it quickly, trying to ignore the prickle of excitement at finally talking with someone else about the plan Ryder and I came up with over beers one night. Summer's still talking, but my mind drifts back to a time when Ryder wasn't sick, and we were young and stupid, planning our futures without a goddamn care in the world.

"It'll be perfect, bro. I'll relocate my branch of Crawford to the island, we can buy out an office building by the beach with your adventure tours on the main floor and my offices up above."

"You're assuming Mom and Dad will let me out of working for the business," I say to my brother after cracking open two more bottles of beer. "They're pretty set on us both taking over some day."

"Fuck that. You don't wanna be there, and no offense, man, but I'm way smarter than you. I'll handle Crawford Books, you take all the hot tourists out on day trips."

"Thanks, asshole, you make me sound like a total douche."

Ryder just shrugs. Piece of shit.

"Just calling it like I see it, bro." He grins.

I miss that grin. I miss him.

We never did get to plan out our futures in any more detail because the next week Ryder was diagnosed with aggressive acute myeloid leukemia and our entire world shifted focus onto his health. Dreams were forgotten in lieu of trying to fight the evil disease that ravaged my twin brother. In fact, the only other time we talked about my idea for an adventure tourism company was on what turned out to be the worst night of my life. We fought about it, tarnishing the dream forever.

"Summer, this looks great. I'm still figuring out the details of what I want to do, so can we maybe revisit this sometime soon?"

It's a total cop-out, and I don't give a fuck. The woman in front of me is nice, friendly, and offering me an opportunity I don't think I would ever pass up if things were different.

She looks at me curiously for a minute, and I struggle not to shift restlessly under her scrutiny. "Sure. That's fine."

Her lunch comes over at the same time as mine. At the same time, the door to the café opens, and I see Paige walk in. My eyes are fixed on her and the instant she sees me, hers widen ever so slightly behind her glasses.

"You know what, I think I'll take my lunch next door and make Mila take a break." Summer stands up and picks up her plate. Paige has made her way to our table, and Summer leans over to give her a quick hug. "Hey Paige, you should join Wyatt for lunch. I'm abandoning him."

Paige looks at me, chewing on her lip. "I do not mean to interrupt your discussion."

Summer just waves her hand, and I try to smile reassuringly. Every fiber of my being wants Paige to sit down. Her nearness is intoxicating in a dangerous way.

"Nah, it's fine. I was just bombarding him with all the things my guests are wanting from me. I'm trying to convince him to partner with me for his new company."

Paige cocks her head to the side and looks at me inquisitively. "I was unaware that your business was so close to opening."

Am I reading too much into her words or does she look hopeful? "It isn't, not really. I'm still in the information gathering stage. Summer was just giving me some good ideas on what to offer if I ever get to that point."

"Alrighty, I'm going to just leave you two. Bye!" Summer walks away, flashing an enigmatic smile.

I stand up and gesture toward the counter. "Can I buy you lunch?"

Finally, Paige smiles back. "I do believe I am in debt to you and should be paying for yours instead."

"That's crap. You don't owe me anything," I reply, shoving my hands into my pockets. Hands that are itching to reach out and touch her.

"Then perhaps it is thanks that I owe you. For what you did the other day."

I can't resist the urge to tease her. "Thanks for the kiss? Because I'm pretty sure you started that, so I really should be thanking you."

Thank fuck, she laughs. "Fine, I acquiesce."

"Great." I grin. "Now what can I get you for lunch? You will join me, right? Eating alone sucks."

"I find eating alone to be quite productive at times." Paige pushes her glasses up on her nose, and I chuckle. Ever the pragmatic Paige.

"Yeah, fair enough. But I'd really love your company today."

That earns me a soft smile and a quick nod, and we head up to the ordering counter. She makes her choice, and thankfully, doesn't protest when I drop a twenty on the counter and pay for her food. Her order is ready quickly and we manage to fill half an hour without touching or talking about the kiss anymore.

Being around her again, feeling her vibrant, yet calming energy, and engaging her beautiful mind causes all my reasons for needing to avoid Paige to fizzle into thin air. I should be anywhere but here, but with her is the only place I want to be.

I walk her back to the store, and when she opens the door for me, I take the invitation and walk inside. She flips the sign on the door back to *Open*, then heads to the counter to drop off her things.

"Plans for the weekend?"

She blinks at me, her lips slightly apart, begging to be kissed. It takes superhuman restraint not to walk over, pick her up, and set her on the counter and devour her.

"Undecided. A fellow bookstore owner in Vancouver has invited me to attend a historical fiction conference, but I have not confirmed."

"What's holding you back?"

"A myriad of things. Transportation, coverage for the store, accommodation. I am not a fan of last-minute plans, as they always feel rushed and not properly thought out."

What comes out of my mouth next is the very epitome of not properly thought out. "It just so happens I was heading to the mainland for a couple of days. Why don't we go together?"

It's an outright lie, and my hand comes up to scrape through my hair, landing on the back of my neck.

"Together? Do you mean carpool?"

"I have a floatplane reserved."

More lies. But thank fuck for money because if she somehow agrees to this insanity, I'll be calling in some favours and opening my wallet.

"That sounds expensive. I would need to examine my budget to see if I can afford such extravagant transportation."

"It's already paid for. All you have to do is join me."

She's hesitating and I don't blame her, this sounds crazy, even to me. But I push forward. "My family knows someone who owns a hotel in Vancouver, they can hook us up with a second room for you." At least that part is true. A good bottle of wine and I know Dad's friend, Bert, will find a couple of rooms for us at the Fairmont. "It's no big deal, really. I'll be busy with my plans during the day while you're at your conference, but maybe we can go for dinner or do something in the evening. What do you say?" It comes as no surprise that I'm mentally crossing my fingers that she'll agree. The opportunity to spend time with Paige away from her store is beyond appealing to me. Visions of taking her out to dinner, walking down the streets of Gastown at night, holding her hand, *kissing her again*...I want, no, I need her to say yes.

"Are you really asking me to go to Vancouver for the weekend with you, Wyatt?" Paige's hands are clenched tightly together in front of her, and I finally give in to what I've wanted to do ever since she walked into the café. I walk over, take her hands in mine, and stare straight into her eyes. She blinks nervously and clears her throat, but I can see the excitement brimming under the surface.

"I most definitely am, Paige."

CHAPTER TEN

Paige

"I should cancel."

"You absolutely should *not* cancel."

I drop down onto my bed next to Summer, who is patiently folding shirts I have been tossing haphazardly her way. When she texted me earlier asking if I wanted to go for a walk, I suppose she read something in my reply. Ten minutes later she was on my doorstep, inviting herself in, and is now attempting to help me pack.

"You want to go to the conference, don't you?"

How she is so calm is beyond me. My insides are spinning faster than a roulette wheel, and I have not been able to sleep for more than a handful of hours since I somehow agreed to go to Vancouver with Wyatt.

"I do. But I could just go on the ferry, and I'm sure I could stay with my colleague that is providing the ticket for the conference."

Summer arches her brow at me. "You really want to stay with a complete stranger, in their home, instead of in your own hotel room? Come on, Paige."

She has a point. Up until now, Seth and I have communicated via email and one phone call. His invitation for me to use his extra ticket for the conference was unexpected, but I am truly excited for the opportunity to attend. Still, spending the night at his home, when I have never met him face to face, feels incredibly uncomfortable.

"You make a valid argument, Summer." I let my head drop forward to stare at my hands, feeling exposed by my irrational anxiety.

Summer drapes her arm around my shoulder and tugs me in for a side embrace. "It's okay to be nervous. I can tell Wyatt means something to you, even if you don't quite know what that is yet. But try to relax and enjoy yourself."

"I kissed him."

"Wait, what?" Summer straightens up and takes my shoulders, forcibly turning me to face her. "You kissed Wyatt? When? Where? Why?"

"Would you also like to ask who and how?" I reply, letting sarcasm lace my tone. Summer rolls her eyes, quite accustomed to my dry sense of humour.

"Spill the beans, Paige."

"Yes, the day before the author signing event, at the bookstore, and because I wanted to." I rattle off my answers, counting them on my fingers.

"And?" Summer nudges me. "How was it?"

My tongue darts out to lick my suddenly dry lips. How was it? How do I answer that? Summer is aware of my lackluster experiences with physical intimacy in the past. How do I tell her that kissing Wyatt was like the earth cracked open under my feet? That everything I thought I knew about myself, my wants, my desires, has been thrown into the air and fallen down like confetti, chaotic and messy.

"It was nice."

"Nice?"

I nod, keeping my eyes downcast. "Yes, nice. Quite satisfactory, in fact."

"Paige, honey, I'm gonna need more than that. Come on. Talk to me." Summer's voice is gentle, kind, understanding. If there's anyone I feel I could speak with about the tumultuous feelings inside of me, it's Summer.

"I don't entirely know how to express my thoughts on this. Kissing Wyatt was extraordinary. I have been, quite frankly, overwhelmed by the sensations I experienced in that moment."

Summer's smile is enigmatic. "You have feelings for him."

I frown at her quizzically. Grasping subtext is hard for me sometimes. "I don't understand what you mean. Of course I have feelings, I find him interesting and attractive to look at."

"No." Summer gently shakes her head. "You have *feelings* for him. You like him. You want to be with him, romantically."

"That would be pointless for me to feel, Summer. He will be leaving Dogwood Cove soon, that much is certain. For me to allow myself to develop the type of feelings you are indicating would only end in loss and pain for me."

"He might be leaving soon, but he's also made it seem like he wants to come back. Why else would he be considering opening a business here? Besides, what about the pain of never opening yourself up to possibility? You're one of the smartest, most self-assured people I know. Be brave, Paige."

Be brave.

Those two words have taken up residence in my head, thanks to the countless times I have repeated them to myself since Summer left me alone with a packed suitcase and reassurances that she and Ashley would manage the store for the weekend. I may not know Finn's girlfriend Ashley that well, but Summer worked with me temporarily when she first moved to town, so I do have faith in her. If she believes this trip is a good idea, then it is.

But standing on the dock looking at the tiny plane that is meant to carry Wyatt and me to the mainland, I start to question that faith.

"It's perfectly safe, I promise."

Wyatt's smooth voice rolls over me. When I first arrived, I didn't see him and surmised I had arrived early. That was clearly an error on my part, as it allowed time for me to ruminate on one crucial piece of information I have withheld from Wyatt until now.

"I've never been on an airplane before."

To his credit, Wyatt doesn't let his surprise at my admission show, but I am certain he feels it. What independent woman in her thirties hasn't been on an airplane in their life? Thanks to my overly concerned parents worrying about my health, the answer is — me.

"I'll be beside you the entire time. It's safe, and who knows? You might actually enjoy it."

Wyatt takes my hand as he speaks and slowly leads me closer to the floatplane. A man waiting there gives Wyatt a nod. I assume this is our pilot because he takes our bags and loads them into the plane as Wyatt turns me to face him.

"I won't let anything happen to you, Paige. I promise."

It is completely illogical, and there is no reason for me to believe him, but I do. Wholeheartedly. Which is why I let him help me step up and into the plane, I let him adjust the headset over my ears so we can talk to each other, and I let him take my hand in his as the plane begins to taxi over the water. He flinches slightly when I squeeze tightly as the plane lifts up into the air, but when I mumble an apology, he simply covers our hands with his other one and rubs his thumb across my knuckles comfortingly.

Eventually, I am able to relax, and to my surprise, Wyatt is right, I do enjoy the flight. It's over far too soon, and the landing in Vancouver is a lot bumpier than I would have liked. But the views crossing the Georgia Strait are spectacular and seeing the coastal mountain range come closer and closer is awe-inspiring.

After we disembark the plane, Wyatt leads us to a parking lot and straight to a car that he unlocks with a fob from his pocket. When he notices my curious expression, he comments, "I paid for long-term parking when I came over to the island."

The drive to the hotel is blessedly short, but it's when we pull up to the valet station at the Fairmont Waterfront hotel that I realize I had no idea we were staying *here*.

"Wyatt, this is uncomfortable for me to admit, but I truly cannot afford a place like this, nor do I wish to be indebted to you."

Wyatt ignores me, climbing out of the car, coming around, and opening my door. I ignore his hand when he reaches in to help me step out. "Did you hear me? I appreciate your efforts, but this cannot stand."

Finally he speaks. But it isn't what I expected him to say. "Paige. Can you do one favour for me this weekend?"

I ponder what he could possibly want from me. "That depends on what the favour is," I reply.

He shakes his head ruefully. "Can you not worry about the money? I've got it covered, I promise. I don't want to get into the specifics, I just don't want you to worry about it. Just enjoy yourself. It means a lot that you're here with me, even if we are here for different reasons. I'm looking forward to spending time with you, and I hope you can relax and have a good weekend with me. That's all I ask."

Well. How on earth am I supposed to formulate a response to that?

Wyatt doesn't seem to need one, as after a second or two of staring at me, he appears to reach an internal decision. Taking my hand in his, he grabs the handle of my suitcase, places his bag on top, and walks toward the entrance of the hotel. He checks us in quite quickly, and soon we're in the elevator heading up to the tenth floor. I have yet to say a word, and truly, I am still at a loss on what to say to Wyatt. It's not that I wish to appear ungrateful, I simply am unused to having someone bestow lavish gifts on me, such as he is doing. And while I appreciate that he does not see them as gifts, I do.

We reach our adjoining rooms, and Wyatt hands me the key card for mine.

"Would it help if I let you pay for dinner tonight?" he asks, his voice light with humour. But I can see something more significant brewing beneath the surface. Something that tells me I am most definitely not alone in feeling overwhelmed by the intensity of whatever is growing between us. Which makes my necessary reply all the more awkward.

"It would, however, I have already made arrangements to have dinner with my colleague who provided the ticket for tomorrow's event. Could we perhaps meet for breakfast tomorrow instead?"

Wyatt's face falls, but he recovers quickly. I see a mask of indifference cross his features, a shield of sorts. It almost seems as if he feels rejected somehow. "Yeah. Sure. I'll just grab some room service. See you in the morning."

The door closes behind him and I stay in the hallway for several minutes, trying to process what just happened. The chime of my phone breaks the spell, and I look down to see a message from Seth instructing me where to meet him. I unlock the door to my room, deposit my suitcase, and after a quick moment in the bathroom to freshen up, I'm on my way out again for dinner. Something makes me pause outside Wyatt's door, but I don't linger.

That would be a mistake.

A short while later, I realize my previous statement was incorrect. The real mistake turned out to be coming to dinner with Seth. The man is insufferably boring. He's at least twenty years my senior, divorced, and clearly under the mistaken impression that this evening was intended to be more than dinner between two fellow bookstore owners. I immediately dissuaded him of the notion that there was a romantic element to our meeting when he attempted to draw me in for an embrace. What followed was an awkward, stilted conversation that I marginally improved by consuming copious amounts of wine.

When at last our dishes were cleared and the bill was present-ed, I quickly pulled out my emergency cash and placed it on the table before standing up.

"Thank you, Seth, it was enlightening meeting you in person. I do appreciate the invitation for the conference. Perhaps I shall see you at one of the panel discussions tomorrow. Goodnight."

I hurry out of the restaurant before he can reply, instantly regretting my over consumption of wine as my gait is unsteady and my eyesight somewhat blurry. When I return to the hotel, it has only been an hour since I departed. I make my way to the bar situated off the lobby and order a gin and tonic. Perhaps imbibing more liquor is not wise, but I need something to distract myself from thinking about the fact that Wyatt is here, upstairs, alone.

But I consume the drink far too quickly and find I'm still thinking of it. Of him.

I'm thinking of him as I ride up to our floor in the elevator.

And as I walk down the hall toward our rooms.

And as I try to swipe my key card over and over, cursing the damn light that will not turn from red to green, until the door opens suddenly and I tumble forward into strong arms.

"Paige? What the hell?"

I blink up at his face. "You're fuzzy."

"You're drunk."

I nod. "Correct. I have consumed a lot of alcohol tonight." I push past him and into what I now surmise is his room and not mine. That would explain the key card not working. I kick my shoes off and moan at the luxurious feel of the carpet beneath my bare feet.

"This is high quality carpeting."

"I don't give a fuck about the carpet. Here, drink this." Wyatt presses a glass of water into my hand and guides me to sit down on a chair. I watch as he seats himself on the bed across from me. I squint to make sure I am not seeing things, but no, he is truly shirtless. All of his glorious muscles, and what I can assume is a highly intricate tattoo, are on display. But they — he — is too far away for me to touch.

I want to touch him.

I want him to touch me.

I want him to give me my first orgasm.

It's only when he lets out a strangled noise that I realize I am speaking out loud and not merely making observations in my head.

"Paige, I'm not going to lay a finger on you tonight. You're drunk, you don't know what you're saying."

I think he's shaking his head, but the truth is, my vision is so blurred, it is as if I'm not wearing my glasses at all. Experimentally, I take them off, then put them back on. No difference. Interesting.

"Perhaps my inebriation is making me bold enough to tell you my desires. What if tomorrow my courage goes away? Will you still act on my request? I would like to learn what it is about orgasms that has my female friends so infatuated with them. My experiences thus far have been lackluster, to say the least."

"Holy shit," he groans, dropping his head down to his hands. I wish to feel his hair between my fingers, so I attempt to unsteadily make my way over to him. As soon as I'm within reach, his hands come to rest on my hips and his head tilts up to look at me. "Paige," he murmurs, and I place a finger on his lips.

"I touched you first. It's fine." I let my hands drag through his hair, enjoying the low moan of pleasure that brings from him. To his credit, he stays frozen, his hands doing nothing more than stabilizing me with his firm grip on my hips. My fingers travel down to his shoulders and around to his chest, where I trace the outline of what I've deduced are wings. "I have long admired tattoos. I realize that may go against what many think of me and my character, but I admire the art form. The permanency of decorating your skin with something important."

His hands cover mine and lift them off his chest to hang by my side. "You shouldn't let other people's opinions or expectations stop you from doing whatever you want."

"I don't."

"Good."

The temperature in the room seems quite high. Or perhaps it is just me. Looking somewhat blindly over my shoulder, I manage to find the glass of water and bring it to my lips to drink, only to have it partially spill down my front.

"Okay, come on tipsy, let's get you back to your room." I watch as Wyatt opens a door that I realize must connect our two rooms, then he wraps an arm around my waist and leads me out into the hall. When we're in front of my door, he holds out his hand, and I obediently hand him my key card. He opens my door, deposits me on my bed, then goes and unlocks the connecting door on my side.

"That's just in case you need anything in the night, okay? You've had a hell of a lot to drink, and I want to be able to check on you. That's all."

I nod. Suddenly the alcohol is catching up to me and I want nothing more than to climb into the bed and sleep. Standing up, I lift my sweater over my head and drop it to the floor. My hands go to the button on my pants before I realize Wyatt is still here. Our eyes meet after his lift from my chest, covered only by my bra.

"So, I'll see you in the morning," he says hoarsely.

"Yes," I reply.

We stand there, eyes fixed on one another for a moment more before he pivots and walks into his room, gently pulling his door mostly closed.

I finish undressing, collapse onto the bed, and immediately fall asleep.

CHAPTER ELEVEN

Wyatt

Did I sleep last night? No.

Did I get up twice to make sure Paige wasn't sick? Yes.

Did I spend way too long watching her sleep, smiling at her cute little snore? Also, yes.

Did her words run through my head on constant repeat, like a digital billboard in Times Square? Fuck. Yes.

She wants *me* to give her an orgasm. Her first orgasm, if I understood her drunken rambling correctly. Honestly, all the blood rushed to my dick when she started talking about me touching her, so I could be mistaken. Yet somehow, I don't think I am.

At five, I gave up on sleeping, and after a final check on Paige, I headed down to the hotel gym. A fast five mile run and some weights got the blood pumping but did nothing for the nervous energy built up inside of me, knowing I'm going to have to face her in a few hours. Will she even remember last night? She was pretty drunk, so who knows. I know I won't forget it any time soon.

I get to the restaurant downstairs first, so I order us both some coffee while I wait. When she enters, I can't avoid the smile that curves up my face. She's dressed extra formal today, except on her it's less uptight and more of a sexy librarian style. The black pants hug her slender frame, and the light-coloured shirt is tailored to fit her perfectly. Her hair is swept up in a braid that drapes over one shoulder. Eventually she finds me and makes her way over to our table.

"Wyatt. I believe I owe you an apology," she says as soon as she sits down, and I instantly reach my hand over to lay it across hers.

"You don't. And I won't accept one."

"But my behaviour last night," she starts to tug her hand away, and I tighten my hold.

"You had some drinks, Paige. We all say things when we're drunk."

Her cheeks colour. "That's the problem. I do not recall everything I said, which unnerves me. But I do recall touching you. And I fear that was too forward of me."

"Trust me, it wasn't. I respect that you go for what you want in life, Paige." I flash her a wink. "Especially when I'm the thing you want. The only reason I didn't let it go any further is because I didn't want to take advantage of you in that state. But if you hadn't been drunk, this would be a different type of breakfast."

Her brow furrows. "In what way?"

"We'd still be in bed."

Paige's jaw drops open. She recovers quickly, and I keep my chuckle to myself.

"So, breakfast, then you're headed to your conference until late afternoon, right?"

She nods.

"Awesome. Well, assuming you don't have plans again tonight, can I take you out for dinner?"

It takes a moment, but eventually Paige nods and I release her hand. "Great. I'm guessing you need some greasy breakfast foods to fight off the hangover?" I give her a teasing grin, but to my surprise, she shakes her head.

"Actually, there is no evidence to suggest fatty foods assist in the alleviation of hangover symptoms. I drank two glasses of water when I woke up, took a cold shower, and some Tylenol. I'll be fine with some toast and fruit."

I hide my smile, but damn, I love her brain and her no-nonsense approach. "Okay, then. Toast and fruit it is."

Over breakfast, I cajole Paige into telling me what led to her inebriated state last night. When she tells me how this jackass Seth assumed they were on a date, my back goes up. But she calms me down surprisingly fast when she explains how she dealt with him. Still, the idea that she might see him again today rubs me the wrong way. But there's nothing I can do.

When we go our separate ways, her to the conference, and me to do God knows what to fill the day, seeing as I don't *actually* have anything to do in the city, I pull her into my arms and press a light kiss to her forehead.

"Have fun."

Paige blinks up at me, a small smile cresting her lips. "I shall do my utmost to enjoy learning about the latest trends within historical fiction, but I suspect the panel on World War II dramatic sagas may not be entertaining in that sort of way."

Once again, her sense of humour hits perfectly. "I guess not. Then instead of saying 'have fun,' how about I say 'have an enlightening time.'"

"Much better."

Then to my surprise, Paige lifts up and swiftly kisses the corner of my mouth before joining the crowd of people walking into the convention center.

And like the sap I'm turning into with her, I stand there on the sidewalk and watch her go.

For dinner, I take her to one of my favourite restaurants in Vancouver. It pays homage to the city's obsession with sushi, but with a West Coast twist. Over salmon rolls, Paige fills me in on the conference, and the animation on her face while talking about the panels she attended is mesmerizing. But when I hear the name Seth, my focus snaps into place.

"What did that fucker want?"

"Wyatt, your protective tone is unwarranted. Not only was Seth perfectly respectable, but you and I are not in a relationship. You have no right to become defensive on my behalf. Did you or did you not dislike that type of behaviour when Ethan displayed it at Hastings?"

Well, shit. Her chiding hits me on several levels. But what shocks me is the part that stings the most — hearing her say we're not in a relationship. We're not, but I want to be. And that is startling for me to acknowledge.

Setting down my chopsticks, I make sure I have Paige's attention when I reply. "I'm sorry. You're right, I was out of line. Then again, as I told you that night with Jeffrey Asshat Morgan, no one deserves to be disrespected, and after what you told me about your dinner last night, I was worried that he wouldn't take no for an answer." I pause, trying to figure out how to word the next thing I want to say. In the end, I decide the truth is the easiest. "And we may not be in a relationship, but I care about you, Paige."

That shuts her up.

After that, the conversation shifts to more neutral topics. It surprises me how much we have in common. For someone who claims to have lived a sheltered life, Paige's intelligence and natural curiosity have created a woman with varied interests and opinions. I don't remember the last time I had this kind of a connection with a woman. Normally, the priority is getting naked as fast as possible. But with Paige, I want to know more about her. I want to know everything.

When we leave the restaurant, we set off along the cobble-stone streets of Gastown. The old steam powered clock blows, and we both pause to listen to it.

"What's something you've always wanted to do but think you never will?"

Fall in love.

My gut response to Paige's question is one I keep to myself. It's a secret I don't plan on ever sharing. The truth is, I know love and a family is not for me. Even if there wasn't the whole fear of losing someone I care about again, there's also the fact that, with Ryder being my identical twin, the chance of me having cancer in the future is higher than normal. And there is absolutely no way I could subject the person I love to the grief that comes from losing their partner.

"Get a pet."

Paige cocks her head at me quizzically. "That's a very generic response. I must admit, I am surprised; I expected you to name an extreme sport or some sort of dangerous activity. May I enquire why you feel you will never have a pet?"

I shrug. The reason is similar to the one behind my secret response. "Losing people you're close to is really hard. I imagine losing a pet would be hard, too. Not the same, but still. Why set myself up for that grief?"

Paige tucks her hand into the crook of my elbow. "That seems a very pessimistic outlook, yet I can understand your reasoning. However, I must point out that death is a fact of life. Coming to terms with mortality is important if you want to achieve true peace in life."

"What's your impossible thing you've always wanted?" I ask, hoping to change the subject. Paige is dangerously intuitive.

She seems to think about it for a while, so I'm expecting her response to be something deep and esoteric.

"Get a tattoo."

I come to a stop and face her. "Really? That's your big thing?"

"Yes. I have always wanted a particular quote as a tattoo, but I doubt I will ever be in a position to actually have it completed by a trustworthy artist."

My mind starts working instantly. "Do you trust me?"

"You keep asking me that, have I not proven by now that I do?" Well, fuck, that feels good to hear.

"Then give me two minutes."

Her brow crinkles slightly, but she nods. I pull out my phone and send off a quick message to Rocco, the tattooist I have always used. He's a great guy, and if there's anyone I would pick to put their hands and their ink on Paige, it's him. Thankfully, he's more than happy to do me a favour and says we should come right over. His shop is a couple of blocks over, so when I pocket my phone, I give Paige a huge grin.

"Are you ready?"

"For what?" she asks cautiously, but I see excitement dancing in her eyes.

"For your impossible thing. My guy Rocco will do your tattoo right now."

For a moment Paige just stands there, her mouth gaping open and closed like a fish. I start to worry that I made a mistake, and she's going to refuse. Then slowly, she smiles, and it's the biggest, brightest smile I've ever seen.

"Let's go."

I give her my answering grin and we head off down the street to Rocco's shop. He's technically closed, but he unlocks the door and ushers us right in. Introductions are made, and we all head down a short hall lined with incredible artwork, to Rocco's room.

"Okay, pretty lady, what am I putting on you? Wyatt says this is your first time."

Paige nods eagerly. "Yes, this will be my first, and most likely, only tattoo. I know exactly what I want. Do you have some font styles I could look at?"

Rocco hands her a small album and her hair cascades around her face as she pores over it. He looks at me, eyebrows raised, and an unspoken message passes between us. Yeah, she's hot. Yeah, she's with me, so *back off*.

Pretty soon they've decided on a font, and I'm burning with curiosity to hear what she wants done. But then she lifts her shirt and turns to the side and I'm struck dumb by the smooth expanse of skin she's revealing. My mouth legit starts to salivate at the idea of running my hands and my mouth over her body.

"Could you please write the words *I have never known love* across my ribs right here?" Paige gestures to her side, up high. With one final glance at me, Rocco switches into professional mode and rolls his stool closer. His gloved hands come to her side as he turns her slightly, and goddamn, do I hate that he's touching her there first.

"Yeah, we can do that. Depending on how big you want it, it can wrap around to the front or back."

Paige turns to me, blinking innocently. Her shirt is lifted so high, I can see the barest hint of lace cupping her tits. "What do you think, Wyatt? Should it curve to the front or the back?"

"Front, definitely front," I croak out, earning a subtle laugh from Rocco. The asshole knows exactly how much I'm affected right now. I take a step back as Rocco gets Paige situated on the table, and I use the opportunity to turn away slightly and adjust myself. This is becoming a problem, and frankly, I'm shocked Paige hasn't noticed my physical reaction to her. Or maybe she has and she's got the decency not to draw attention to it. Either way, I need to fucking get it under control.

"Okay, you ready to get started?" Rocco asks, and Paige's hand shoots out to grab mine.

"Yes."

I give her a reassuring smile. "It only hurts for the first little while, then your endorphins kick in and it's no big deal."

Rocco laughs from his position by her side. "Don't lie to her, man, you know that only happens on bigger pieces." He lifts the needle from her skin and looks at Paige. "This is gonna hurt, pretty lady. But if it ever gets to be too much, just say so and we'll take a break. Although, honestly, this is only gonna take maybe half an hour."

Paige's head bobs up and down. "I'm fine. Lets get this done."

I use my free hand to gently tuck some hair behind her ear that had fallen into her face. It's an intimate gesture that reminds me of last night when she was pressed in between my legs. Fuck, if she hadn't been wasted, that night would have gone a lot differently.

Clearing my throat, I force my thoughts elsewhere. "So, what's the meaning behind the quote?"

"It is a line from one of my favourite books."

"Yeah? Seems a bit depressing for your one and only tattoo."

I shoot a glare at Rocco because even though I was thinking the same thing, his reply has Paige's face falling slightly. She composes herself and keeps her eyes on me. "The character who says it is someone I resonate with. I understand and appreciate his emotions. Romantic love isn't for everyone and that's fine. You can live a perfectly satisfying life with only platonic relationships."

Even Rocco doesn't have a retort for that, and he dips his head down and gets to work. I squeeze Paige's hand and try to reply.

"I think it's perfect that you're getting something that has a lot of meaning for you. That's what your first tattoo should be, in my opinion."

I see her face and shoulders relax. Guess that was the right thing to say. Rocco finishes quickly, and I try to slip him some money, but he waves me off.

"Consider it a favour."

Paige also tries to protest, but Rocco's Italian spirit comes through and he stubbornly refuses, ushering us out onto the street after giving Paige her aftercare instructions.

Back in the cool night air, her hand finds mine once again and our fingers thread together naturally. We walk in silence for a little while before I ask the question I'm dying to ask.

"Are you going to tell me what book the quote is from?"

"It's...a romance novel. I doubt it would interest you. The author, E. Peake, is fairly new to writing, but her books evoke such emotion. This one is called *Trouble Me*."

I file that away in the mental box of *random facts about Paige*.

"And the guy who says this — he doesn't believe in love? How does that work if it's a romance novel?"

Her lower lip tucks between her teeth. "Well, he eventually falls in love. But only once he finds a partner who meets him where he is emotionally: comfortable living his life alone and outside of the societal norms. Someone prepared to love him exactly as he is and makes him feel as if he finally belongs somewhere."

I don't stop to think about why I'm reacting to her explanation this way, I just act, pulling her in to my arms and kissing the shit out of her.

It's rough and passionate, and she meets me stroke for stroke. Our tongues are dancing together as if they've done this a hundred times. She lets out a little moan and my hips tilt into her, letting her feel the full effect she has on me. We stay here, locked

together with our arms and our mouths, for what feels like forever, but in reality is probably only a minute or two before the
sounds of people walking past us filter into my consciousness
and I force myself to take a step back.

"Damn, Paige."

"We should go back to the hotel," she gasps. I take in the
burning fire in her eyes, her flushed cheeks, her heaving chest,
and my dick throbs in the confines of my jeans. For a woman
who says she doesn't believe in romantic love, she sure is letting
herself feel lust.

"Let's go." I wrap my arm around her shoulder and tuck her
in close to my side, needing as much contact as possible. Neither
one of us says a word as we walk the streets of Vancouver back
to the hotel, but the energy around us hums with something
so heady, so powerful, it's staggering. That kiss back at Rocco's
tattoo parlour almost made me come unhinged. I am dangerously close to finding a wall to push her up against and sliding
my hands down the front of her pants. And knowing that she's
equally as turned on? Just means my hotel room needs to be a
lot closer, right now.

When we finally get into the thankfully empty elevator, I turn
and cage her in against the wall, my hands coming to either side
of her head.

"There's no alcohol running through your body tonight,
Paige, so I know you'll mean it completely. What do you want?"

Her eyes dilate and her tongue darts out to lick her lips. "I
want you, Wyatt."

"What do you want me to do," I growl.

"I..." she falters, and her head starts to tilt down. Instantly my hand cups her chin and nudges it back up, so her eyes meet mine.

"No way. Don't second-guess it. What. Do. You. Want."

"I want to have sex with you. I want you to make me orgasm." Her voice is strong this time, and what I needed to hear is loud and clear.

"Good girl."

Chapter Twelve

Paige

The way my body reacts to those two words defies all logic. The area between my legs has its own pulse, it is throbbing so strongly. I ache with the desire to feel his hands touch my body, touch me there. I'm quite confident that if anyone is capable of helping me reach the pinnacle of desire, it is Wyatt. And with every passing second, I grow more and more eager to experience it.

When the elevator doors open, Wyatt pulls me down the hallway to his room. One swipe of his key card and the door is open, then his hands are on my waist, spinning me around and pushing my body against the now closed door. Perhaps I should feel trapped with his body so close to mine and nowhere to go, but I don't. If anything, I feel free. Freer than I ever have.

"I'm gonna make you come like this," Wyatt growls into my ear as one hand moves to the front of my pants and makes quick work of opening them. I want to tell him to slow down, I don't want to miss a single second, but at the same time, it feels excruciating, waiting for his touch. When his thumb finally grazes the stiff nub of nerve endings between my legs, I shriek, my hands coming to clutch at his shoulders. Sensation like I have never experienced is zapping through my body. It's uncontrolled, wild, and reckless — everything I am not.

Wyatt is relentless. His lips plunder my neck while his fingers dive between my slick folds. My hips start to move of their own volition, seeking his touch. He chuckles against my skin.

"Easy there. Let me do this."

His low voice seeps over me like molten lava, calming my nerves and agitating my senses.

"Please, Wyatt." My voice is breathy, and for the briefest of seconds, I wonder if I'm going to need my inhaler. But the thought disappears when Wyatt slides a thick finger inside of me, causing me to lift onto my toes with a gasp.

"Fuck, Paige, you're so fucking tight and wet. You're ready, aren't you, baby?"

"Yes. I am. Oh God, don't stop doing that." My hips are still moving around on his finger, desperately seeking something, I don't even know what. But Wyatt must know because his free hand comes to my waist and holds me still. Then he slides a second finger in to join the first, and twists slightly, putting pressure on a place I didn't realize existed in me.

Out of nowhere, a cascade of indescribable physical responses floods my body and mind, shutting out anything other than the intense pulsing of the muscles between my legs. When the throbbing clench turns to a lighter flutter and eventually stops,

I'm shocked to come back to awareness and feel Wyatt's fingers still drawing circles around my sex. There's a slickness down there that I have never had before. My eyes open and I see a satisfied smile on his face, and something akin to wonder in his eyes. An expression I am certain is mirrored on my own face.

"That was an orgasm," I state bluntly, immediately cutting eye contact with him because of course it was. He's very aware of that fact, seeing as it is likely a far more frequent experience for him.

"That was fucking spectacular," is his low reply, causing me to glance back up at him.

I clear my throat, and push my glasses up my nose. Why I am overcome with nerves after what he just did is beyond me, but here I am. "I did not expect it to happen that quickly, to be honest. I am pleasantly surprised."

My confession doesn't make Wyatt laugh as I wondered if it would. If anything, his gaze darkens until his eyes appear almost black in the dim light coming from one lamp beside the bed. His hands go around me and he easily lifts me into his arms. My legs dangle awkwardly, until he slides one hand down my thigh.

"Wrap your legs around me, Paige. Feel what you do to me."

I do as I'm told, a moan escaping my mouth when the new position brings our pelvises together. I can feel the rigidity of him pressing against the fabric that separates us.

Wyatt drops me on the bed and I scramble back until I'm leaning against the pillows, my motions jerky and uncoordinated. But he is anything but that as he slowly lifts his shirt off, revealing his glorious torso. I don't remember that much from last night, but I do remember the fluttering of my heart when I saw his chest.

He goes to the top of his pants and his hand stills. "You're still with me?"

I nod vigorously and his lips quirk up in a small smirk. Excruciatingly slow, he undoes the button and slides down the zipper. He bends over and pushes his pants and underwear down at once, obstructing my view until he stands back up.

"Oh my," I gasp, my mouth falling open. His erection juts out, long, thick, rigid. He walks around to the side of the bed closest to me, and I blink rapidly, certain I'm seeing things. "What's that?" My hand stretches out tentatively, toward the metal barbell sticking out of the tip of his penis, but I snatch it back before I make contact.

Wyatt lets out a deep chuckle. "You can touch it. It's an apadravya."

"But why?" I sputter, completely shocked that he would do that to himself, yet also fascinated by it. "Piercing your genitalia must have hurt immensely. What was your motivation for doing so?"

Wyatt's hand wraps around the base of his length and he slowly starts to rub himself, sending a fresh wave of wet heat to my sex.

"Because I wanted to? And because when I use it the right way, it can make sex feel even more mind-blowing, especially for the woman I'm with." He winks and my hand lifts up to wipe away the drool I am petrified is dripping from my mouth. I've read about this type of arousal, this intense sexual attraction, but never once did I expect to feel it myself.

Wyatt lifts one leg up and comes to kneel on the bed. "You've got too many clothes on, Paige."

I scramble to sit up and go to lift my sweater over my head, but his hands stop me.

"I want to do that."

He takes the hem of my sweater in his hands and pulls it up and off of me, revealing my bra and the bandage Rocco applied to my tattoo just an hour earlier. So much has changed since then; it feels like a lifetime ago that I let Wyatt take me for my tattoo. His hands skirt around the edge of the bandage before coming to cup my breasts. His thumbs graze my nipples, making them stand up stiffly. He leans over and licks a path over the top of one breast, down the valley between, and up the crest of the other side, all while gently squeezing with his hands. I never realized my breasts were so sensitive, so erogenous. Then again, everything is different with Wyatt.

Everything.

His lips come back to my neck, landing there with soft, open-mouthed kisses that I accept eagerly. But I am impatient. I want more. I suspect what I experienced against the door was but a mild version of what Wyatt is capable of, and I want it all. When he shows no sign of moving further with undressing me, I take matters in my own hands, arching my back so I can reach the clasp on my bra, sliding it off my shoulders, and dropping it to the floor. Wyatt lifts his head up and his eyes travel down to my breasts. A part of me wants to cover them, but the bigger, bolder part that he is unleashing within me wants to feel his mouth there again.

"Will you kiss me here?" My hands come to where his just were, cupping my breasts. He grins at me, a wolfish, lust-filled smile.

"You have no idea how fucking sexy it is hearing you ask me to give you what you want."

Wyatt lowers his head but keeps his eyes trained on me as he slowly wraps his lips around my taut peak. The warm heat of his mouth engulfs my breast, and his tongue swirls around my nipple, teasing it even stiffer than it already was. He plays my body expertly, switching sides, alternating from sucks, to gentle nips, to wide licks. It's never the same, I can never anticipate what he's going to do next, all I can do is let go.

Finally, he reaches for the fastening of my pants and makes quick work of finishing the job he already started of undoing them, breaking away from my breasts to slide my pants and my underwear down my legs, leaving me completely bare.

"You're so gorgeous."

There's nothing in his tone to indicate he is anything but serious and I can't deny it feels wonderful to receive the compliment. I place my hands on his sides, and tug gently to encourage him back up to my head so I can kiss him. Once again time is suspended and I'm lost in the feel of his lips on mine, his tongue plundering my mouth. But he eventually shifts onto his side, and reaches behind him, producing a foil package.

I try not to seem overly curious as I observe him opening the package and rolling the condom onto his penis. I still have yet to touch him, not because I don't want to, but because I am far too nervous and excited for what comes next. Silently he reaches for a tube, and squeezes out a clear gel-like substance which he rubs on top of his covered penis. He comes back to lean over me, the muscles of his arms bunching as he holds himself up.

"Are you ready?" He lowers to his elbows, and shifts onto just one so his hand can come up and stroke the side of my face. I nod quickly, but sense he needs more reassurances.

"I'm not a virgin, Wyatt, merely inexperienced. I have had two other sexual partners, but neither were as arousing as you have already proven to be. I am more than ready. I feel I may combust from the fire burning within me."

"Fuck. The way you talk. You. You're just... Fuck, Paige." As he says my name, Wyatt begins to slide his covered erection into me slowly, moving the tip in and out a few times before going deeper. I'm grateful for the slow pace, and for the lubricant he applied because as much as I want to feel all of him, I'm tight, and unused to the intrusion. But then he's in, and his piercing hits my inner walls, sending instantaneous spasms throughout my core.

"Oh my God," I moan as my body arches up from the over-whelmingly heady sensations flooding me. "Wyatt!"

"I know. Jesus, Paige. You feel amazing, squeezing the shit out of my cock like that."

His rough, gritty, dirty words have a direct affect on my arousal, sending pulses of need through me. He starts to pump his hips and we quickly find an intoxicating rhythm. The room is filled with the sounds of our lovemaking, his grunts, my gasps, the slap of our skin. Wyatt reaches down and lifts one of my legs up to just under his arm and the change in angle causes me to shriek out his name. I'm climbing higher and higher, like I'm on a roller coaster about to crest at the top before plummeting down. I both want to hit that release and never want this climb to end.

"Come for me, Paige."

With a strangled cry, my body responds to Wyatt's command instantly, my orgasm hitting full force, my sex pulsing around him. He groans out my name as his thrusts become chaotic, until with one more push he freezes and unloads into me. He drops down onto his forearms, releasing my leg, and peppers my face with wet kisses as our hearts both pound from the exertion.

Wyatt climbs off of me with one final kiss, and I watch him walk to the bathroom. Moments later he returns and holds out a wet cloth with a questioning tilt to his head. Unsure what he means to do with that, I simply nod. To my shock, he proceeds to gently wipe me clean, placing soothing strokes over my sensitized flesh. The towel is tossed to the floor and he climbs into the bed, pulling me into his arms, simultaneously lifting the duvet that was folded back to cover us.

"I feel I should thank you for...that. For what you did. What you made me do." My words tumble out of me, but Wyatt just chuckles and tightens his arms around me.

"Trust me, no thanks are necessary. That was just as amazing for me as I think it was for you."

"Really?" I ask incredulously, lifting my head to look at him. He tilts his chin down to meet my gaze.

"Yeah. Sex is pretty much always good, but sex with you is fucking phenomenal. Whoever made you think you weren't made for this was dead wrong."

My head slowly lowers back to his shoulder, a different kind of satisfaction creeping through me. Idly, I let my fingers trace the outline of the wings on the feminine body that runs down the middle of Wyatt's strong chest. "Will you tell me about this? Having now experienced my first tattoo, I cannot imagine the fortitude it would take to sit through a session long enough to complete such a work of art."

Wyatt shifts on the bed, moving me slightly. "It's a Valkyrie. The legend is they were maidens chosen by the god Odin to go into battle and choose from the dead who would be worthy of a place in Valhalla. My twin, Ryder, was always obsessed with Norse mythology. I used to tease him relentlessly about the video games he would play all the time when we were teenagers. Now I wish I had just played them with him when he would ask."

"You have a twin?" I interrupt, my mind racing with this revelation.

"I...had a twin. He died twelve years ago. Cancer."

"Wyatt. I'm so very sorry." I bring one hand up to cup his face, wishing I could wash away the pain I see etched there. "You don't have to talk about it if it's too painful."

"No, it's okay. It's good to talk about him. Anyway, after he died, there was no question in my mind that he went straight to heaven, whatever that may look like. And I like to think he had a fiercely beautiful woman escorting him there. And since I can't let him have all the glory, I decided to hold that belief close to my heart."

The emotion with which he speaks of his brother fills me with longing. I cannot begin to imagine the depth of connection he must have felt with his twin. To have that connection severed is a great tragedy. Nonetheless, a small part of me is envious that he got to experience that type of relationship at all.

But it becomes apparent that Wyatt does not want to dwell on this subject as he rolls me over until I am straddling his waist.

"Wanna see how good it feels like to come like this?"

The day after our return from Vancouver is the monthly book club meeting. Thankfully, the woman Mila invited to talk about...well, who knows what, had to postpone. Normally, I use the days leading up to the event to prepare a list of discussion questions, but this time I was understandably distracted by both my nerves leading up to the trip with Wyatt, and naturally, by what occurred that night.

I admit to being mildly disappointed that Wyatt did not initiate further sexual relations when we woke up the next morning. However, upon self-reflection, I had to acknowledge my body required some time to recover. The flight home was far less stressful for me, likely due to Wyatt's hand stroking my inner thigh and his lips kissing my shoulder and neck the entire time, thoroughly distracting me from the breathtaking view.

We arrived back in Dogwood Cove twenty-four hours ago. I have not seen Wyatt since he dropped me off at home with a spine-tingling kiss. A kiss I am still thinking about as I move around my house, preparing for my friends to arrive, as it is my turn to host. I have debated in my mind whether or not to tell my friends about my sexual enlightening, and have not yet arrived at a decision. Part of me wants to tell them how I finally understand their reactions, the other part of me wants to keep what transpired between Wyatt and I a secret.

But that choice is taken away from me as soon as Serena walks into my house. She's the last to arrive, and as soon as she sees me, she drops her coat on the back of my couch and lets out a whoop.

"Halle-freakin-lujah, our girl got some!"

"Some what?" Abby asks, walking in from my kitchen with a glass of wine. I start to answer, trying to deflect from Serena, but as she is prone to do, my dear friend barrels on ahead.

"Orgasms! Look at her, she's glowing. You have to tell us everything, Paige!"

I frown slightly at Serena's exuberance, even as I fight my own inner cheer. "It's impossible for me to glow, Serena. I don't know what you're seeing."

We've made it to my small living room where the rest of our group awaits. They are all looking at me with expressions that range from curiosity to excitement.

"Is she right, Paige?" Mila asks eagerly, and I give in to the inevitable.

Sinking down on the couch beside her, I pick up my glass of wine and compose myself. But I am unable to entirely hide my smug smile as I reply, "If Serena is indicating I have now experienced the spectacular ecstasy that accompanies a true orgasm, then the answer is most assuredly *yes*."

CHAPTER THIRTEEN

Wyatt

"Strathcona is the oldest provincial park in BC."

This isn't the first random factoid Paige has sprung on me since we started our walk an hour ago. Like I did with the other pieces of information she shared, I smile. She's nervous, and I don't blame her. The last time I saw her was when I dropped her off at home after our fucking phenomenal weekend in Vancouver. We never did talk about the orgasm situation; hell, I don't even know if she realizes I knew she'd never had one before. I sensed that she needed a little space, so I stayed away yesterday, only sending her a couple of texts so she didn't think I was ghosting her. But this morning, I wanted to see her, so I sent a message asking if she wanted to go for a drive to the park. Her reply came back quickly, and here we are.

"Is that right? We're walking through history, that's cool," I reply, taking care to keep my tone relaxed. The trail grows a lot steeper ahead, but it also widens enough that I can move up beside her, and I take her hand. It feels natural to be with her like this, which if I'm being honest, makes me feel a little uncomfortable. I don't remember the last time I felt this close to a woman, or even the last time I spent this much time with the *same* woman, outside of a bedroom. But with Paige, I want more. She's slowly filling in the holes in my soul that I honestly thought would ever fill. With Ryder's diagnosis, and the increased risk to my own health, I wrote off the idea of ever having a partner in life. But Paige is somehow making me question that. Which is a little terrifying.

Suddenly, Paige pulls me to a stop, snapping me out of my spinning thoughts. When I look at her, my heart plummets. She's pale and breathing oddly, with pursed lips.

"Shit, Paige. What's wrong?"

"Inhaler. Front pocket." She gasps out the words as I guide her to a rock to sit down. I fumble slightly but find the blue device I assume she's talking about. She grabs it from my hands, shakes it, and puts it to her mouth as I drop to my knees in front of her and dig around in my pack for some water. My mind is racing; I can feel panic creeping over me like a darkness. I push it away, willing with everything I have for Paige to be alright.

"Thank you."

My eyes fly up to meet hers, and thank fuck, her breathing appears to be slowing down.

"Are you okay? Do we need a medevac? What do I do?" The words tumble out of me, but Paige puts her hand on my shoulder. When I cover it with my own, I notice her tremble.

"No. I'll be fine in a minute. I'm sorry, Wyatt. I thought I was okay, but that's the way it goes with asthma. I believe that last uphill stretch was too strenuous for my lungs."

"Don't apologize. I'm the one who should be sorry. I pushed us too fast. I screwed up, Paige. Fuck."

I drop her hand and stand up abruptly to pace up the trail and back, needing a minute to let the adrenaline coursing through my veins stop pumping. I want to hit something; hell, I want to hit myself. How could I do this to her? How did I not notice she wasn't doing well? My hands come up to tug through my hair as the panic turns into self-flagellation.

"Wyatt." Her voice is stronger, which calms me slightly, but I don't stop pacing.

"Wyatt, stop. Look at me."

I slowly turn to face her.

"I'm okay. This isn't your fault. I know my body, and I know my limits. If I felt we were going too fast, or the hike was too hard, I could have said I needed to slow down. But I didn't. Sometimes my asthma catches me by surprise."

She stands up and I hurry over to her, holding her hips as she seems a little unsteady. The grateful smile she gives me just makes me feel even more shitty.

"See? I'm fine."

"You're not fine, Paige," I growl, my fingers digging into her.

"I will be. I used my inhaler, and with a little bit of a rest, I'll be good to keep going." The way she pats my arm is probably meant to be reassuring, but it's not.

My eyebrows hit the sky at her words. "Are you fucking kidding? We aren't hiking anymore, we're going home. I'll carry you to the car."

"Don't be ridiculous."

Great, now she sounds angry. I guess it's better than the scared, breathless voice that asked for her inhaler earlier. Still, I'm not being ridiculous. There's no goddamn way I'm going to put her in any more danger. I couldn't help Ryder, but I can help Paige. That comparison may be totally unfair, but I can't avoid it.

"I'm not. You just had an asthma attack, Paige. Your...your fucking breathing was screwed up."

Paige's hands come to her hips, and man, if looks could kill, I would be a smoking pile of ash right now.

"Thank you for stating something I have known my entire life. My breathing was screwed up. Such an eloquent way of describing a *mild* exacerbation."

"Don't use fancy words on me right now, please." I swallow down my anger at myself and look at her. I mean, really look at her. And she seems okay. "You scared me," I say hoarsely.

Paige's shoulders drop and I am unable to look away from her face, so I see it soften in understanding. She steps in toward me and my hands lift to circle her waist, tugging her forward until she falls against my chest. The reassuring thump of her heartbeat against my body slowly soothes me as we stand there, nothing but the sounds of nature around us.

"I promise you, I am truly alright." Her words are mumbled against my chest, and I tighten my hold on her. "Although, if you squeeze me any harder, I may suffocate."

I release her with a small laugh. "Sorry."

When she steps forward and lifts my hands to circle around her back, I laugh again, and the last of my stress lifts away as we hold each other.

"I didn't say stop hugging, I just needed you to not squeeze so tightly." Her voice is steady, calm, and light. Thank God.

"You got it."

After a few more minutes, she looks up at me, chewing on her lower lip. "Okay. You're right, we should head back to the car."

My eyebrows draw together and I frown. "Are you okay? Do you need your inhaler again?"

She shakes her head, her eyes widening. "No, no. I'm fine. Well, my lungs are fine. As fine as they can be, I suppose. That is to say, they're never truly fine, but right now they —"

My lips find hers, effectively stopping her rambling. I keep it quick, nothing more than a chaste peck, really. But it works. She opens her eyes and lets out a soft sigh.

"Thank you. I could feel my nervousness taking over."

"Why are you nervous?"

She's silent for awhile, then she squares her shoulders and looks me dead in the eyes.

"Because I want you to take me home and make me come again."

Well, goddamn. Apparently all it takes to get me hard is hearing Paige tell me what she wants. Every time she does it, her growing confidence is even sexier than the time before.

The trip down the path goes a lot quicker than it did when we were going up, despite me constantly checking in with Paige. After the third or fourth time of her telling me to stop asking if she was okay, I give in and trust her to say if she needs a break. We reach my car and I toss our bags in the back, buckle in, and peel out of the parking lot so fast the tires spin out on the gravel.

In the seat next to me, Paige is laughing, and it's the most beautiful sound. "Wyatt, speeding is not necessary."

"That's what you think," I grumble, lifting her hand to my mouth to press a kiss to it. "You can't tell a man you want him to make you orgasm and then not expect him to want to do that as fast as possible. Now come on, distract me with more facts about Strathcona Park."

Thank fuck for weekday traffic, or the lack thereof because we make it back to Dogwood Cove in record time. I drive straight to my house and park on an angle in the driveway. Striding around to her side of the car, I open the door and lift Paige out and straight over my shoulder in a fireman's carry, answering her shriek of surprise with a light swat on her ass.

"Wyatt!"

"Stop wriggling. I need my hand to open the door."

"Then put me down!"

"Not happening."

I manage to get the front door unlocked, slammed shut, and locked again, all with holding her in place with one arm. I head straight up the stairs to my room, and only then do I lower her to the ground. She starts to glance around, but I capture her chin and make her look at me. With her focus where I want it, I lift her thin shirt up and over her head. Her hair is falling out of the braid she has it in, so I gently untangle the elastic and run my fingers through it, letting it fall free. My lips find her collarbone as I kiss a path across from her shoulder to the column of her throat, then down, between the swell of her breasts, until I circle her bellybutton.

"What...what are you doing?"

My head tilts up. "I'm kissing you. Then I was going to take off your pants and make you come with my mouth. Any questions?"

"N-n...no..." Paige brings her hands to my shoulders, and I can't figure out if she's pushing me away or holding me in place. "I've never experienced...that."

"You've never had a guy go down on you and stroke you with his tongue, suck your clit into his mouth, and fuck you with his fingers until you're dripping down his face?" I'm pushing her limits with the dirty talk, I realize. But something about knowing I'm not only the first guy to give her an orgasm, but also the first guy to ever taste her is turning me into a possessive, sex-crazed, Paige-obsessed maniac. I need her, and she needs this.

"I can honestly say no, I have never experienced that." Her husky voice is making it hard for me to focus.

"Then I guess I get to be the first."

"You've been the first for a few things." Her eyes are wide, showing her honesty and vulnerability.

"I know, baby. You told me that night you were drunk in my room. I'm honoured I was able to give you your first orgasm. Those other guys were idiots and didn't deserve you."

She doesn't reply, but the smile on her face and the soft way she strokes her hand down my face is enough for me. I lean back in, and press an open kiss to her navel as my hands pull her leggings down over her ass, kneading my fingers as I go. Paige tangles her hands in my hair and *this* time I know she's holding me in place. When I glance back up at her, there's no mistaking the arousal and the anticipation on her face.

I help her step out of her leggings, then I slowly kiss my way back up her thigh until I reach her lace-covered sex. Her fingers tighten, then relax as I press a kiss over the lace in the middle of her legs, breathing in her unique musky scent. It's addictive. I want more. My fingers curl under the edge of her panties, and I start to tug them down. Still moving slowly so she can stop me anytime, but something tells me she won't. She wants this as much as I do. Her hands move to my shoulders as she steps out of her underwear and kicks it to the side, and then she's bare to me. In that moment, the importance of this experience hits me again.

"You're stunning, Paige. Everything about you amazes me. And knowing that you trust me with this, with your body, I want you to know I don't take that lightly."

The light in her eyes shines through her glasses, filling me with something indescribable. Unable to wait another second, I take my first taste with a pass of my tongue up her slit. Paige gasps and her upper body bows over, her hands coming back to my head. My fingers find her ass and squeeze as I take up a relentless pattern of licking and sucking, flicking her clit with my tongue, then thrusting in and out. I discovered that Paige goes crazy when she doesn't anticipate what I'm going to do next. Which means there's not any repetition to my actions, I'm alternating and changing my approach with every moment.

"Oh God, Wyatt," she moans, and I can hear her panting. I lean back, just far enough to make her look down at me, and I lift two fingers up to her mouth.

"Suck."

She opens her lips and I push my fingers in. Her tongue swirls around them, making me grunt as my dick strains against the confines of my hiking pants. I pull back, lower my hand and slip my fingers between her folds, coating them in the moisture there.

"Are you ready?" I ask hoarsely. She nods vigorously and that's all I need. I slide my fingers in and curl them around to find her G-spot. When she lifts onto her toes and her hands forcefully push my face in closer to her, I know I've hit my mark. My mouth latches onto her clit and I suck firmly, and that's all it takes for her to scream out my name as her sex convulses around my fingers, flooding me with everything she can give.

Her orgasm goes on in waves, and I stay right there with her through it all. For a woman who lacks experience, Paige is one of the most passionate and sensual women I've ever met.

Eventually, I feel her limbs relax, and with one final kiss to her clit, I slowly pull my fingers out, catching her as she sags against me. I manage to stand up, lift her into my arms, and place her on my bed before stripping off my shirt and pants, leaving my boxer briefs on, and climb in beside her. I love how long it takes her to come down from an orgasm. To me, that just speaks to the intensity of what Paige feels every time, and that's fucking hot. She lets go fully, allowing herself to be immersed in sensation, and watching her slowly drift back to reality is beautiful.

She is beautiful.

Chapter Fourteen

Paige

The cliche of feeling like you're floating on air has always eluded me. Until now. For several days, I have felt light, happy, and free. If I stop to think about the cause of my ebullient mood, I start to question it. Therefore, I am choosing to simply enjoy, and deal with any repercussions later.

Today is a day I have been looking forward to for some time. I've shut down the shop for the day, and I will be out in the grassy area of the town square for the festival-style fundraiser and adopt-a-thon Mila and Jackson have organized to raise funds to open an animal shelter in town. Utilizing his connections as the town vet, Jackson has brought in staff from several shelters in other parts of the island who are bringing adoptable animals to showcase. There are games and vendors who paid to display their items for sale, and there is a concert later tonight.

Mila and Jackson roped all of us in to help with the final stages of organizing and setting up the event, which is how I find myself carrying crates containing bunnies to the space designated for the Victoria Regional Animal Shelter. The volunteer thanks me as I set it down, and I dust off my hands, then turn to go to my next task, only to be frozen in place from the sight in front of me.

Wyatt is carrying an adorable tan coloured puppy that is nestled in comfortably in his arms. He's unaware of me, but I watch his every move. The sight of this man carrying a puppy — the man who is coming to mean more to me than I expected — causes my heart to flutter in my chest in an alarming way. My hand lifts up to rub my chest, as if to ease the strange sensation, but then he dips his head down to kiss the puppy's nose and a sound escapes me.

"Damn girl, that man is all kinds of fantasies come to life. He's like a walking, talking advertisement for the perfect guy." Serena drops her arm over my shoulders, startling me from my ogling.

"Hush, he'll hear you," I admonish, looking quickly to Wyatt, who has stopped at a shelter's set up to deposit the puppy.

"I'm just saying. You need to lock that down. You're happy, Paige. Happier than I've ever seen you. It's subtle, but it's there and it's because of him."

Serena walks away, leaving me to obsess about her observation. I never thought of myself as unhappy, but she's right. Lately, I have felt remarkably cheerful.

I walk over to Wyatt, who is now bent over the fenced-in area where the puppy he dropped off is up on its hind legs, licking his hand.

"That puppy certainly likes you," I comment, coming to stand beside him. He twists to face me with a grin, and my hand reaches up to push a stray curl of hair back from his forehead.

"She's freaking adorable isn't she? So chill, too." He looks back down at the puppy who is now sitting down, but still watching him, her head tilted to the side. "You should get her."

"What? Me?" His comment surprises me, but then I reach my hand down, and the puppy instantly starts licking my palm. "I can't..."

Wyatt straightens and turns to me, pressing a kiss to my cheek. "Sure you could. Hi, by the way."

"Hi." I keep my eyes focused on the puppy. She truly is a sweet-looking little dog, and part of me can envision her curled up on a bed beside me at the store. A warm hand comes under my chin and tilts my head up. Wyatt's blue eyes are warm, and open, as he leans in and kisses me on the lips softly.

"Okay you two, break it up. There's work to do." Mila's loud voice interrupts us. Wyatt backs away, but takes my hand in his as we turn to face her.

"Wyatt. I know you're new here, but you're part of the crew, so let's get to it. Ethan and Reid are setting up the VIP section for Nash's concert, can you go and help out?

Wyatt looks from Mila to me, shock evident on his face. "Nash, as in, Nash Parker?"

Mila nods proudly. "Yeah, his drummer is friends with my brother. Nash and his girlfriend fell in love here during the

Summer Solstice Festival last year, so they were happy to come back and help with the fundraiser."

Wyatt kisses me once more, briefly, then heads over to where Ethan is carrying a metal fence panel. My eyes follow him, greedily drinking in the way his jeans hug his backside, the narrow taper of his back to his trim waist. I know the muscles that lay beneath the fabric of his shirt, and that memory has my tongue darting out to lick my lips.

"You've got it bad, girlfriend."

I glance over at Mila, a frown furrowing my brow. "Got what?"

"Him. You. You guys. Seriously, if the sparks get any hotter between you two, we'll need a fire extinguisher."

I feel my cheeks heat up at her words. "I apologize if we made you uncomfortable. I am unaccustomed to having a relationship that involves public displays of affection, so I must admit I'm not certain where the line of propriety is."

"Oh honey, I'm sorry. I didn't mean to embarrass you," Mila takes my hand in hers and I can't help but notice how much I prefer the feel of Wyatt's rough, strong, large hands to hers. "I'm just so happy to see you like this. You seem so relaxed and happy."

"Why does everyone keep saying that? First Serena, and now you. Was I truly that unpleasant to be around before Wyatt?" I can't keep the hurt out of my voice. My reaction is unexpected. I'm not prone to strong emotions, but when it comes to how others perceive me, my sensitivity is deep-rooted.

"No, no, no. Oh my God, Paige, no. We love you, just the way you are and always have. I'm sorry, I didn't mean it like that at all." Mila's voice is full of remorse, and she has taken hold of both my hands, forcing me to stand facing her. "Let me see if I can explain it better." She takes her lower lip between her teeth, her eyes searching me as I stand there stiffly. I love Mila as a good friend, but her scrutiny feels extremely uncomfortable right now.

"It's fine, Mila. You don't need to —"

"Shush. You need to hear this. Because you're incredible, and I don't think you realize that. You're beautiful, smart, kind, funny, and so damn strong and confident, it's easy to forget that you're also human, and you can't always tell when we're teasing out of love. I don't mean that Wyatt makes you better because you weren't good enough before. You were — you *are* — I mean. But since he came into your life, you've changed — in a good way. I wish I knew how to describe it, but it's like you're settled and more open. Oh man, I'm making a mess of this, I'm sorry."

"I don't know how to feel about a man changing me," I answer honestly. "I've always felt quite content with myself and my life, even if I don't quite fit in everywhere. I realize I'm different, and I don't always respond to social cues appropriately. But here, with all of you, I felt as close to belonging as I ever have. It's...It's unsettling to hear that perhaps I am better with Wyatt than without. Because what happens when he leaves?"

"Is he leaving?"

"I don't know. I would assume so? We haven't ever talked about what we're doing or what the future may hold. Truthfully, I have been avoiding the topic, as the uncertainty of what his feelings might be causes me a considerable amount of worry. Content to simply enjoy the moment, if you will. However, your observations are making it painfully clear that I must address the situation soon."

"Paige…" Mila starts, but I can tell she is unsure how to proceed. I drop my hands and try to give her a reassuring smile.

"It's alright, Mila. I understand what you are saying. And I know you have the best of intentions. I am easily overwhelmed and confused by relationship dynamics, specifically intimate and romantic ones, due to my complete lack of successful experience with them. But I shall navigate this. And I will do my utmost to retain this new *relaxed and happy* way of being, even after he is gone from my life."

"I wish you wouldn't say that like it's a foregone conclusion. You're good together. Don't you want to maybe try and make it last?" Mila sounds hopeful, and I wish I could say I felt the same.

"Yes, of course, I have thought about that. But I suppose I have not allowed myself to truly envision it to the point of discussing it with Wyatt. I'll consider doing that." Even though the idea of doing so gives me a strange nervous feeling in my stomach.

Mila gives me a small smile just as someone calls her name.

"You should go. The day will be a big success, I'm certain of it."

"Thanks, Paige. I love you, you know that, right?"

I smile stiffly. For all that I care deeply about my friends, professing love for them is a strange concept for me. "I know."

After she walks away, I turn back to the pen of dogs behind me. Stooping low, I pick up the tan coloured girl Wyatt was holding earlier and snuggle her into my chest.

"You are sweet, aren't you?" I murmur into her fur as she licks my chin.

"She looks really good with you."

I feel Wyatt's presence as my body responds to his voice, shivers dancing up my spine. His hand comes to my lower back and a kiss is pressed to the side of my head. These small affectionate gestures are so meaningful to me. Perhaps Mila is right, and I should talk with him about whether or not he sees a future for us.

"Why don't you take her? It was your dream, wasn't it?" I ask, referring back to our conversation in Vancouver, the same conversation that led to my tattoo.

Wyatt chuckles. "Yeah, but I can't take on a dog right now. Not with my lifestyle and how much I travel for work."

My heart plummets at the word travel; at the same time, a dawning realization hits me.

"I just realized, I don't even know what you actually do for work."

Wyatt looks away and shifts on his feet, as if my statement makes him uncomfortable. "Oh, really? I could've sworn we talked about it. I'm a...consultant, I guess you could say. For businesses looking to expand."

I nod slowly. Something about his answer doesn't ring true, but I have no grounds on which to doubt him.

"Seriously though, Paige. You should get the puppy. Look at how happy she is with you."

I look down, and sure enough, the small dog has fallen asleep in my arms. Her lips are curled up slightly as if she is smiling.

"Okay, I will."

We end up missing Nash Parker's concert because the shelter is packing up before then. Instead, Wyatt and I take my new companion to the local pet store to buy some supplies before heading back to my house to get her settled.

"Perhaps her name should be Sandy based on her colouring?"

Wyatt flashes me a skeptical look from the driver's seat. "Come on, you can be more creative than that."

He's right, and I slump back down. We have been debating names for the puppy ever since we left the festival this afternoon. Now it's growing dark and we've arrived at my house. I shouldn't be nervous, it's hardly the first time Wyatt has been at my house, we've spent several nights together so far. But after my conversations with Serena and Mila at the festival, I feel somewhat unsettled. As if there is unfinished business between Wyatt and I, and tonight I need to find out his intentions. If there is pain and rejection in my future, I need to know now, before I fall deeper for this man.

Because Mila and Serena's observations have made one thing abundantly clear. I have fallen for Wyatt James. I will not claim it to be love, but a strong emotional connection is forming. The question is whether or not that connection goes both ways. And that question is the root of my unease.

Wyatt climbs out of the car and opens the rear door, grabs the bag of dog food and the bag of other supplies, while I carefully get out of the car with the puppy in my arms. We make our way to my front door where I hand Wyatt my key and he lets us in. I sit down on the living room floor and put my new friend down to explore.

"You might want to show her where to use the bathroom first," Wyatt calls out from my kitchen.

"Smart plan." I stand up and scoop up the puppy, walking quickly through to my back door. As soon as I set her down on the grass, she squats.

"Good girl," I coo, picking her back up. Inside, Wyatt has set up a bowl for water and for food, and is busy taking the tags off of the toys and the dog bed. I lean against the kitchen counter for a moment, just letting the comforting feeling of his presence sweep over me.

He belongs here.

That's a dangerous thought. Especially when it is followed up with a question. *What if he doesn't want to stay with me?*

"How about Polly?"

Wyatt's suggestion pulls me out of the spiral of overthinking I was headed down. A small yip comes from the puppy, who has discovered a toy and is now running around the kitchen with it in her mouth.

"I like it. Polly."

Wyatt crouches down, and Polly runs up to him with the toy flapping on either side of her mouth. He scoops her up and presses a kiss to her head. "I have to admit, it's a selfish suggestion. Polly is what I always wanted to name a dog if I got one."

I sink down to the floor and lean against the counter, content to watch Wyatt play with Polly.

"Why that name? Is there meaning behind it?"

He's silent for a moment before answering. "It was my grandmother's name. We were really close when I was young. She died when I was twelve, from cancer." He draws in a ragged breath before finally lifting his eyes to meet mine. "The same cancer that killed Ryder."

The grief lacing his words is underscored by the vulnerability and pain I see in his expressive eyes. The importance of what he has just said isn't lost on me, the impact that may have on Wyatt's future. Suddenly, the conversation I wanted to have ceases to be a priority. My sole focus is on offering whatever comfort I can.

Going onto my hands and knees, I crawl over to Wyatt and settle in his lap, wrapping my legs around his waist. Without saying a word, I cup his face and pull him in for a soft kiss. His breath escapes him in a long exhale, as if sharing his pain with me has unburdened him of a great weight. We stay like that, holding each other, for several moments of silence. The feeling of Wyatt's chest rising and falling underneath me is soothing with its strong, steady movement. But then, something shifts. His breathing accelerates, and showing his significant strength, Wyatt manages to stand up with me still in his arms.

"Are you okay leaving Polly out here unsupervised?" There is a sense of urgency in his tone. A raw, pulsing need. I recognize it for what it is. A desire to escape from the pain.

"I'll put her in her crate," is my quick reply. Thankfully, the shelter gave us the crate she was accustomed to traveling in, and it is easy to get Polly settled in there. As soon as I am done, Wyatt lifts me back into his arms, this time cradling me as a groom would his new bride. He kisses me deeply as he walks down the hall to my room and lays me down on my bed.

Any thought of Polly, of my feelings, of Wyatt's intentions — it all fades away. The only thing I can feel is a deep, unending need for his lips on my body, igniting a fire from the smouldering embers that are left every time he touches me.

Chapter Fifteen

Telling Paige about my grandmother, and the hereditary nature of the cancer that killed her and Ryder, wasn't as difficult as I thought it would be. If anything, it lessened my grief slightly, just knowing that someone else was there for me. For no reason other than they wanted to be. That being said, yet again, I didn't tell her the whole truth. I didn't tell her that my risk of developing leukemia is significantly higher. How could I burden her with that? How can I burden anyone with that.

I won't. Especially not Paige. Because the terrifying truth is, I'm developing feelings for her, stronger than I should be.

Last night, holding her in my arms, I had a dream where I stayed in Dogwood Cove. Okay, so there were also dancing whales and some guy with three arms, but the point is, I woke up feeling happy. Like that could be my future, if I wanted it to be. And I do, but also, I don't. The idea of walking away from Crawford Books and opening myself to the life I've always wanted is tempting. But the idea of disappointing my parents, of not doing everything I can to live up to Ryder's memory, that overrules everything.

"Mmm. Good morning." Paige's sleepy voice brings a smile to my face.

"Hey baby. How did you sleep?"

She turns over in my arms, cuddling into my side. This softer side of Paige, the loose and relaxed woman who isn't holding herself back, this woman is pure temptation. All of our differences disappear in the intimate moments we've shared, and she's simply the woman I'm slowly falling for.

"Surprisingly restful, seeing as your body is a constant source of heat. I tend to prefer a cooler sleeping environment, but your warmth was...comforting."

That makes me chuckle. "I would apologize for being *hot* but I think you like that about me." I wiggle my eyebrows suggestively at her, earning a giggle.

We both hear Polly whine from the kitchen at the same time, and Paige jerks upright.

"Oh no, I forgot about her!" She scrambles out of bed, muttering under her breath as she grabs her glasses and a hair tie.

I get up more slowly, adjusting my morning wood slightly in hopes of it calming down somewhat. When I make it to the kitchen, Paige is standing in the open doorway, encouraging the puppy to go to the bathroom. I make myself busy with the coffee maker, getting two mugs ready, pointedly trying to ignore how domestic this all feels.

After the puppy is fed, and the coffee is made, I carry both mugs back into Paige's bedroom and settle myself against the headboard to wait for her. A moment later, she walks into the room, pushing her glasses up her nose as she approaches the bed.

"What are you doing back in bed?"

"Isn't it obvious?" I ask, then instantly wish I could take back the words. It's so easy to forget how inexperienced Paige is in intimate relationships. Chances are, the two guys she was with before me didn't even spend the night. And when I think back to the times I've slept over so far, we've always gotten up quickly in the morning to go our separate ways. But I remember her telling someone at the fundraiser yesterday that the store would not be open again today, so I assumed we could have a lazy morning in bed. I envisioned introducing Paige to shower sex and showing her how fun it was to be dirty as fuck while getting clean.

I lift the blanket and pat the bed beside me. "Come here."

She slowly walks around to the other side and climbs in, but there's too much space between us. I reach over and pull her into my side, covering her mouth with a kiss. When I release her lips, the nervous look is gone from her face, replaced with a dreamy, satisfied smile.

"We're gonna cuddle, and drink coffee in bed, then we'll figure out what we're doing today."

Her eyes blink open and a small line appears between her brows. "Wyatt, I have to go to the store today."

I can't deny the jolt of disappointment at that. "I thought you weren't opening?"

"I'm not, but I have several online orders to catch up on."

"That's fine, we can do that after we do something fun with Polly. Don't you want to take her for a walk? Maybe down to the boardwalk in Westport?" I don't mean to sound needy, but it probably seems that way. Fuck, who am I, practically begging a woman to spend time with me?

I guess Paige is also surprised by my request as she scoots herself into sitting more upright. I'd rather she was still in my arms, but at the same time, I appreciate the space because these weird reactions and feelings I'm having around her are unsettling. I've never wanted to spend so much time with one woman before. A part of me wants to just enjoy it, enjoy her, and another part of me wants to run away. Thankfully, I'm smart enough to listen to the part that wants to stay.

"How about this. Let's drink some coffee, take a shower, then we can go to the store first, if you want. I'll help you with the orders, if you'll let me choose what we do after."

Finally, she smiles. Thank fuck. I hand her one of the cups of coffee.

"That sounds nice."

Mentally I pump my fist in the air. Like a goddamn idiot. She's got me all twisted around into some messed up version of myself that I don't even recognize. Actually, I do. It's the version of myself I was before Ryder died.

Thinking of him, of the me I used to be, the me I could have been, is a dangerous path to go down, so I set my coffee aside, take hers and put it on the bedside table next to mine, and push her down on the bed. I lower my head and take her breast in my mouth, sucking her nipple through the fabric of the tank top she wore to bed.

"Wyatt!" she gasps, arching her back.

I lift away, only to grab the hem of her shirt and pull it up and over her head. Then my mouth finds her breast again and I lose myself in the taste, sound, sight, and feel of her. I can only hope that fucking her will chase away the ghosts of my past.

Turns out, that was a bad attitude to have before sex. When it was over, I feel wrong. Dirty, and not in a good way. I feel like I used Paige, and that thought makes me sick to my stomach.

We shower separately, and I take the opportunity to make up some breakfast while she's getting ready. Her pleased expression when she walks into the kitchen to see me setting plates with eggs, toast, and fruit in front of her does a lot to reassure me that she wasn't harbouring any negative thoughts toward me. Thankfully, she seems completely unaware of where my head-space was at.

After cleaning up breakfast, we pack up and head out. Paige agrees to head to Westport for a walk first, so I hit the highway, driving the short distance to the neighbouring city. We happen to pass the new location of Crawford Books, and I inwardly wince at the reminder of the secret I'm keeping from her.

We hit the boardwalk and attempt to walk. I say *attempt* because Polly has us stopping every five steps so she can sniff something.

"Is it normal for puppies to be so easily distracted?" Paige asks, but I can tell by the happy cadence to her voice that it's a rhetorical question. In response, I scoop up Polly and tuck her under my arm, taking Paige's hand with my free one.

"Yeah, pretty sure it is. How about we give her a break and get some lunch before we head to the store?"

"That sounds lovely." Paige flashes me a sunny grin, and we make our way over to a food truck parked nearby. The smells coming from it are delicious, and soon we're sitting at a table eating some incredible fish tacos.

"Damn, this is good." I close my eyes as the flavours hit my tongue, and I can't hold back a moan. "Fuck. Tell me this isn't the best taco you've ever had." I open my eyes to see her looking at me, her hand holding a taco halfway to her mouth. "Paige?" I ask and she blinks, shaking her head slightly.

"Sorry. I...I have never seen someone so, umm, happy? No, that's the wrong adjective. So *blissful* eating a taco."

I can't resist the opportunity to ruffle her feathers a little more. "I'll have you know, I'm *always* happy eating tacos..."

Her adorable, confused expression has me biting back a laugh.

"You know what *taco* is a euphemism for, right?"

Paige shakes her head, dropping her gaze down. I reach over and tip her chin up. "No way, baby. No embarrassment around me."

"Easy for you to say. You don't misinterpret innuendo and lack social context for basic sexual topics the way I do." She folds her napkin and sets it down before finally looking in my eyes. "Before I met you, it never bothered me that I didn't understand so much of what my friends would talk about or laugh about. I truly believed that sexual intimacy was not something I required or desired in my life, so why bother learning what all of the jokes or code words meant. I'd had sex, it wasn't that enjoyable, no need to worry about it again. But you've made me throw all of that aside, and now I'm confused. I want to understand, I want to know, but I also don't know what I don't know."

She sounds so frustrated, I can't help myself. I stand up and walk over to her side of the table, sitting down beside her with one leg on either side of the bench.

"Paige, listen to me. Your lack of experience is not a flaw, or a detriment to who you are. It's just who you are. I don't ever mean to embarrass you or make you uncomfortable. Quite the opposite, in fact. I want you to feel comfortable exploring everything with me. I want to be there with you when you learn something new about your body and your sensuality. Because, baby, trust me. It's there. You're sexy, passionate, and more than capable of enjoying sex. And I want to be the lucky bastard who gets to do it with you."

Her lips part with a small sigh, and I lean in to kiss her, drinking in that sigh and everything she has to give me. Her arms come around my neck and I shift closer to her, taking the kiss deeper.

Sounds of people around us break through my concentration. Right, we're on the boardwalk, sitting outside a taco truck. I can't exactly do what I want to do with her right now.

"We should probably go," I murmur against her lips.

"Why?" is her breathy reply.

"Because if I don't stop kissing you, I'm going to want to get you naked. And unless you want to be arrested for public indecency, I don't think I should do that here."

Paige's head jerks back and she blinks rapidly, looking around. "Oh. Yes. You're quite right. I lost track of..."

"Everything?" I say with a grin, and she nods. "Let's go."

The drive back to Dogwood Cove is quiet. I can tell she's thinking about something, but so am I. I'm thinking about how easy it is to get lost in Paige. In the happiness and pleasure I feel when I'm around her.

Back at the store, we settle into an easy rhythm packing orders of books. My memory flashes back to the dream I had, where I stayed in Dogwood Cove. If I did, this could be a regular thing, Paige and I working together, stealing kisses and touches whenever we pass each other. I could get used to that, way too easily. Shaking my head to try and dispel that idea, I walk over to one of the walls that are filled with shelves of books, looking for a particular one for the last order we need to fill.

"Did you mean what you said at lunch?"

Her husky voice hits me. I've never heard Paige sound like that. Pivoting on my feet, I watch her put a book on the shelf in the romance section, then walk over to me. Her hands come to my chest, pushing my back against the shelf behind me.

"What did I say?" I ask hoarsely, my mind scrambled by this seductive side of her.

"That you wanted to help me learn new things."

"Yeah. I meant it."

Her tongue darts out and wets her lips. "Good. Because there is something I've never done, and I want you to teach me."

"Anything, baby."

Paige drops into a squat in front of me, her hands running down my legs to cup the back of my calves.

"Good. Can you teach me how to give a blowjob?"

Chapter Sixteen

My heart is thumping wildly as I wait for Wyatt to respond. I'm not worried about him rejecting me, although, perhaps I should be. No. I trust him when he says he wants to help me, to teach me. And I've experienced his genuine enjoyment in our intimate encounters thus far.

His hand comes to the top of my head and strokes down my hair. I lean into his touch.

"Are you sure this is what you want to do?"

I sense nothing but desire in his voice, despite his words showing some hesitancy. It's clear that he is only holding back out of consideration for me, and all that does is make me even more determined. I don't answer him with words. My hands find the top of his pants and I flick open the button, slide down the zipper, then still. Bringing my gaze back up to meet his, I moisten my lips with my tongue.

"Teach me, please."

Wyatt folds over, bringing his head down to meet mine. He presses a swift, punishing kiss to my lips before widening his stance slightly and pulling his pants down. As soon as his penis, no, this is not the time to use that word — his *cock* — is free, I lean forward eagerly.

"Slow down, baby. Take your time."

Confused, I look up. He takes my hand and brings it to his base. "Squeeze gently, like this." I let him show me, but I'm a fast learner and soon I take over. This time when I lean forward, he doesn't stop me, and I open my mouth to lightly lick the smooth underside of him. The barbell glints at his tip. I'm intrigued as to what that will feel like in my mouth, but first I need to taste more of him. Wrapping my lips around him, I slide his dick in just a bit.

"Damn," Wyatt gently grips the back of my head, not forcing me at all, just holding me. Emboldened, I take in some more of him, calling on all of the romance novels I've read for guidance. But when I try to take him in further, he stops me. "The piercing, baby, it won't feel good if you take me too far."

His consideration at a time like this is touching, and only serves as motivation for me to do the best I can. My hand finds its way up to the back of his thigh, and I move back in, slower this time, until I find my comfortable limit. The barbell hits my throat, and I gag slightly and pull back. He's right, it doesn't feel good if I go too far. But this isn't about me, it's about him. Forming a little suction with my lips, I suck my way to the tip of him until I feel just his crown in my mouth. Then, experimenting, I swirl my tongue around the underside of the crown before lightly flicking the piercing. His head falls back against the shelves as he lets out a barely human sounding grunt.

I'm overwhelmed by how powerful I feel in this moment. It's a heady sensation, knowing he's at my mercy. My hands and mouth start to move in tandem as I suck him back in again, feeling myself start to relax and enjoy what we're doing.

"Paige. I'm gonna come if you don't stop." Wyatt's voice is ragged, and when I cast my eyes up, I see his muscular chest heaving. It's so erotic, I feel my own arousal mounting. His hands come to my shoulders, and I sense that he's trying to let me back away, but I don't want to. "You don't have to —"

I shake my head and continue. Moments later, Wyatt is shouting my name as hot, salty liquid shoots down my throat. I gag but force myself to swallow. It's most definitely not my favourite experience, but Wyatt's enjoyment is evident, and that's enough for me to keep going. When he finally sags back against the wall, I let go of him and self-consciously wipe the corners of my mouth. Wyatt's hands come under my arms and he hauls me up to standing with arms that seem surprisingly shaky.

"Fucking hell." He pulls me in for a deep kiss. "Paige, baby, that was...fuck."

"I trust that means it was enjoyable?" I ask, needing the validation.

Wyatt lets out a choked laugh. "I can barely formulate a complete sentence, baby. That's how good it was."

Inwardly I preen, beyond pleased that my first provision of oral sex was a success.

"Come on. Let's finish up here so I can take you home and repay you for that spectacular experience." Wyatt straightens and slides his hand down to thread his fingers with mine. He lifts, pressing a remarkably sweet kiss to the back of my hand. "You're incredible, Paige. Absolutely incredible."

Wyatt's sweet, romantic words touch a part of me I've always ignored. And for good reason — this part of my heart is vulnerable, unguarded, and inexperienced. Which is why I find myself wondering if what he says could ever be enough. If I could ever be enough. Because reality does not escape me. Wyatt does not live here, and eventually he will leave.

The question remains, will he take my heart with him when he goes? I suppose it is possible. There's no denying my feelings toward him are growing stronger every day. I want him to see me, all of me, not just the parts I share with the world.

Walking behind the counter, I press a few buttons and soon, "A Case of You" starts to play through the speakers.

"Is this Joni Mitchell?"

I nod, secretly pleased that he recognizes the music. Not everyone knows the iconic Canadian singer from the '70s. The fact that he does warms my heart. "Yes, she was my grandmother's favourite. I like to listen to her music while I tidy up in the evenings."

Wyatt inclines his head to me with a soft smile, and we work quickly to finish cleaning up from the orders we put together.

I'll stop at the post office tomorrow morning to send them; for now, I'm eager to go home as well and see what else is in store for the evening.

I don't realize I've started to move until I startle at the feel of hands on my swaying hips. Lips caress my neck, leaving whispers of heat in their path.

"Watching you move like that is giving me ideas. I've never seen you dance before."

My hands come up to rub my upper arms. "I...I don't dance."

"Tell that to those gorgeous hips of yours that were just tempting me with their sway."

I come to a stop, feeling the heat explode across my cheeks. He's teasing. Just teasing. But all it seems to do is underline the differences between us. He's passion, sensuality, freedom. I'm, well, I'm not any of that.

"Paige?" Wyatt turns me in his arms, and I meet his concerned gaze.

"It's fine. I'm fine, just a little embarrassed, that's all."

His lips meet my forehead in a soft kiss. "Baby. You have nothing to be embarrassed about. Seeing you relaxed, knowing that you feel that way around me, it's amazing. You're amazing."

My nervous tension melts away underneath his touch and his words. "Thank you," I say quietly.

"Now, can we finish up and then go to my place? I want to make you dinner."

I look up at him in surprise. "You cook?"

He grins back at me. "Yeah, I cook. One of my favourite things to do when I travel is learn how to make a traditional dish from the area I'm visiting. Do you want pad thai? Cassoulet? Paella? Maybe some ravioli con pinoli?"

"You know how to cook all of that?" My mind is stunned by the idea that he has been to all of those places.

I've never even left Canada.

An insidious voice in my head starts whispering to me. What could I, with my safe, quiet life, possibly offer a man like Wyatt, who has seen the world and lives for adventure? That's a question I'm not sure I want to answer.

At Wyatt's family's summer home, I get Polly settled with a bowl of food while Wyatt pulls out ingredients from the fridge and pantry. When I make my way to join him, he waves me off and slides a glass of wine over the counter to me.

"All I need you to do is sit there and give me something beautiful to look at." He winks, and though I know he means it as a compliment, it's difficult for me to take it as such. Sitting stiffly on the stool, I tug my lower lip between my teeth as I decide whether or not to say anything.

"Okay baby, you're thinking so hard I can feel it over here. What's on your mind?"

With a quick draw of breath, I decide to be honest. "I am not used to being treated as little more than an ornament. To say nothing of the fact that your worldly experiences are intimidating for someone who has never ventured farther than the nation's capital. I cannot help but wonder what I have to offer other than my..." I trail off, mortified. Because as I realized back at the store, I cannot think of a single meaningful thing that I contribute to our dynamic.

"Your beauty? Your kindness? Your intellect? Your humour? Your friendship?" Wyatt stalks around the counter, spins me on the stool, then pins me in with his hands on either side of my body. His eyes are gleaming with fire. "Do I need to go on? Paige, just because I've traveled and you haven't doesn't mean we are unequal in any way that matters. As for you being an ornament, I am so fucking sorry that's how it came across." He lets out a huff of self-effacing laughter. "I was just trying to compliment you. I *want* to cook for you. I want to impress you because you impress me every fucking minute I'm around you."

My mouth falls open. "Oh."

Wyatt lifts two fingers to my chin and gently closes my mouth, then leans in and kisses me softly. "Yeah. So, can I do this for you? Please? Without you overthinking and overanalyzing it?" He kisses me again, once, twice, then pulls back. "And I mean that in the nicest way possible because your beautiful brain is breathtaking to me. But I want you to relax tonight, and just enjoy it. Okay?"

"Okay."

But it isn't okay, not really. Because while he flattered me with his kind words, the niggle of doubt inside of me doesn't go away. I still don't see how two people who are so different, who have lived such different lives, and who are likely going in different directions can possibly make any sort of real relationship work.

Wyatt may not see that, but I do. Nonetheless, I make an effort to do as he asked and ignore my worries for tonight. A handsome man is cooking dinner for me, and I need to find a way to simply enjoy that.

I wish I could say I was successful in tabling my concerns for later, but I wasn't. Not entirely. They stayed with me through dinner, and even when we went to bed. The only time I didn't think about our relationship was when we made love. The rest of the time, the questions and worries swirled inside of me, growing. Festering. Rationally, I know that this happiness Wyatt and I have found cannot last. *We* cannot last without some significant changes in one or both of our lives. He may say he's here to research starting a new business on the island, but that is not enough to guarantee his presence in Dogwood Cove long-term.

Tonight, Serena is hosting book club, and it's the darn sex toy party she and Mila insist on subjecting us to. I'm bringing Polly, in hopes of providing a distraction so that I can avoid any talk of battery-operated assistance. Having only just discovered I am capable of reaching climax with a partner, I have no interest in ruining a good thing by adding in a new element.

I should have known better. My friends are ruthless.

"And this is what I call the 'yes ma'am, you are welcome' because you will be thanking the orgasm gods when you use it." Mae, the woman who arrived with a *suitcase* full of toys and products to share, proudly holds up something that resembles a pink silicone slug.

Serena elbows me, and I belatedly realise I said that last part out loud. Thankfully, no one else seems to have heard, but Serena narrows her eyes at me, and I inwardly groan.

"I think that one looks fabulous, Mae. What does it feel like?" Serena asks innocently.

Our hostess's eyes roll into the back of her head. "Good Lord, I cannot stop coming when I use this. It has gentle suction for your clit, and the perfect amount of stimulating vibrations. Seriously, this baby is a game changer."

Serena turns to me. "Sounds perfect, doesn't it, Paige?"

I scowl in return and stand up. "I'm going to warm up some more food." No one acknowledges me, they're all too fixated on the vibrating cock ring Mae is holding up. Yes, a cock ring. Never in my life did I envision myself here, surrounded by objects specifically designed to enhance sexual encounters.

I wonder if my friends would back off if they knew about Wyatt's piercing.... Perhaps that would be salacious enough for them to stop pressuring me to expand my horizons even further? I don't need toys when I have him. Then again, once Wyatt leaves, do I want to return to my previous state of being, with minimal to no satisfaction achieved from orgasm?

I turn and walk back into the living room and sit down again. I might as well be respectful and listen.

Chapter Seventeen

Wyatt

I know my time off is coming to a close. The emails from work are becoming more and more direct with their requests for my involvement in various things, and although my mother will never come out and demand I come back to the office, my father would. And his email last night requesting to speak today tells me that time has come. My only hope is that I can postpone my return for one more week. I just need to get through the anniversary, then I can go back.

Except.... Going back means leaving Paige.

That shouldn't matter. Truthfully, it comes as a bit of a surprise just how much it *does* matter. We haven't discussed what we are, but I know I'm having fun with her. For the first time, I think ever in my life, I want to spend more time with a woman.

My coffee has just finished brewing when my phone rings. Damn, I wish I'd had the chance to get the caffeine into my system before this conversation.

"Hello, Dad," I say, taking the phone and my coffee over to the couch and sitting down.

"Wyatt. Did you see the latest reports from Alberta? I think we need to speed up the expansion plans in the Calgary area."

My eyes roll upward. It's so typical for him to skip any pleasantries with me and go straight to business. "I'm great, Dad, thanks for asking, how are you?"

My father lets out a huff of exasperation. "No need for sarcasm, son."

When I don't reply, he carries on. "As I was saying, we could use your presence in Alberta next week. Let's see if we can solidify the purchase of that location you found on the west side of Calgary. If we can get the store up and running by the end of the year, I think we should. What do you think about coming home early and meeting me at the office tomorrow to get up to date on everything? We could get you on a plane to Calgary after...you know."

After. After November 8th. After the day Ryder died. That's what he won't say.

I take a sip of my coffee, composing my answer in my head. Because as soon as he mentioned going to Alberta, my entire body felt like it rebelled against the idea of being anywhere but here. But I know if I let emotion fuel my response, I'll get nowhere. "I've still got two weeks off, Dad."

"Right, but you don't have anything planned, do you? You're just hanging out in Dogwood Cove. You could come back early, and then take the rest of your time off later in the year."

Technically, he's correct. But fuck that. I don't want to leave yet. Not if I don't absolutely have to.

"I was actually going to talk to Jacob about going down to St. Thomas and joining him for a week or so." It's a total lie, but it's more believable to my Dad than me wanting to stay here. I hear my father's muffled voice, talking to someone before he comes back to me.

"So you were never planning to come home for Ryder's anniversary."

Wow. I don't think it's possible for him to sound more disappointed in me. Thankfully, I'm used to shouldering the guilt trips. "No, Dad, I wasn't."

"Were you at least going to tell your mother yourself? Or would she spend another year without either of her boys."

Well, that fucking stings.

"I'll call her."

Dad takes in a deep inhale, and lets it out slowly. When he speaks, the disappointment is gone from his voice, and regret is there instead. "Son, when are you going to stop punishing us and punishing yourself? Ryder's death isn't your fault."

It's a damn good thing I'm sitting down because if I were standing, I would have fallen over. That's the first time my father has *ever* said those words to me.

"What...why are you saying that to me? Why now?" I croak out, dropping my head into my free hand. I can feel moisture pooling in my eyes. Goddamnit.

"Because, Wyatt, I'm your father, and I know you. You've been holding on to your grief, and on to some misguided guilt for too long." His voice breaks. "And I've failed you by letting you carry that and not taking it away from you sooner."

"Dad..." I mumble.

"No, listen to me. After the Westport opening, and those few days we spent with you, your mother had it out with me. I don't know how she let it go for so long without telling me to get my head out of my ass. Honestly, she shouldn't have had to. But I'm glad she finally did. I love you, Wyatt, and I miss you. And Ryder dying was not your fault. You are not to blame for any of it. Cancer is. That's all."

I want to yell at him that he's wrong. No, I didn't kill Ryder. I know that. But the way he died. Alone. Scared. And probably thinking I hated him. That's on me.

But no one knows that.

No one knows that the last conversation I had with Ryder, less than an hour before he died, we got in an argument. I stormed out of the apartment we shared and got drunk at a nearby bar. He was on home hospice care, and we knew the end was coming. But he should have had a few more weeks. I should have had time to go home and apologize for being an asshole, and we should have been able to spend his last days together as a family.

Instead, a pulmonary embolism took him without warning. A side effect from one of his many medications. He died quickly, without pain, according to the doctors. Without physical pain, at least. I'll never forget the look of frustration on his face when he yelled at me to come back as I stormed out the door. He couldn't follow me, make me talk to him because he was confined to a bed with monitors and tubes hooked up to him.

"Look, Dad, I can't go to Alberta next week." Thinking quickly, I offer an alternative. "Send Rosemary instead. She's accompanied me enough times, she can handle it. And if there's anything she is unsure of, she knows how to reach me directly. I just...I need more time. Okay? Please?"

There's silence on the other end of the phone. I don't know what my dad is thinking about me suggesting he send my assistant in my place, I can only hope this new version of him, the version that seems to want me to forgive myself, is understanding of my request.

"Alright, Wyatt. If that's what you need to do, I'll always support you. I hope you know that. But can I ask you for something in return?"

My shoulders drop as the tension releases from my body. "Sure."

"When you're ready, can we spend some time together? Just us? Maybe go on a trip out on the boat. Anything you want."

Well, fuck. Now the tears are definitely coming.

"Yeah, Dad. We can do that," I choke out.

"Great. Well, I'll go ahead and talk to Rosemary. Take care, son."

I hang up the phone, sink back against the couch, and let the tears fall. And with each one, I open the floodgates that hold back my memories, the good and the bad. Memories of Ryder, memories of me and my Dad, memories of who I used to be before my guilt and my grief shut me down.

I lose track of time, only half aware of the sun moving across the sky, telling me that hours go by while I'm stuck in my head. An unexpected knock on my door pulls me back to reality.

When I open it to see Ethan, Reid, Jackson, and Finn all standing there, it feels like I'm facing a firing squad. Sure, we all got along and worked well together at the animal shelter fundraiser, but what the hell are they doing at my house?

"Ah, hi guys, everything okay?' I ask, running a nervous hand through my hair.

"Yeah man, Paige told us where to find you. We thought we'd invite you to join us for a trail run," Ethan answers, and it's then I realize they're all wearing athletic clothes. Finn has on a running vest with a water spout attached, and Reid is carrying a set of keys. "Basically, the girls started their book club, and eventually, we guys decided to have poker nights. But then we realized we all suck at poker, so this one —" Ethan jerks his thumb at Jackson "— decided we should start trail running. Every Monday afternoon we head out."

"Don't know what's wrong with a fucking road," Finn mutters, and I stifle my chuckle. He definitely doesn't seem like a guy who's at home in the mountains, but hey, what do I know.

"Let me get this straight. You're here to invite me to go running."

They all nod.

"Right now?"

It's slower this time, but again, they nod.

"Totally out of the blue, on a Monday afternoon, you show up at my house, where you have never been before, to invite me to go running. Is that right?"

Now they're all looking guilty.

"Who put you up to this?" I ask curiously.

"My sister," Ethan mutters, not meeting my eyes.

"Look man, after you guys left before the concert the other night, Mila laid into us. Said you're important to Paige and we need to get to know you. So, here we are. Wanting to get to know you..." Finn trails off. "And damn, that sounds like the most pansy ass thing I've ever said."

This time I don't hold back my laugh, and God, it feels good after the emotions that got stirred up from my conversation this morning with my dad.

"Give me a few minutes to change."

Shockingly, the run turns out to be a good time. The guys set a good pace, and it was a technical enough trail that our minds were occupied with that, and they couldn't bombard me with questions about Paige and I. In fact, the run cleared my head more than I thought it would.

Hanging out with the guys, out in nature, challenging my body, it was good. Exactly what I needed to work through my conversation with my dad, and the responsibilities I've been ignoring. I know I have to go back to work eventually, and I will. Once I get through Ryder's anniversary.

When the guys extend the invitation to meet everyone at the bar later on, it's an easy thing to agree to. As soon as I get home from the run, I shoot a text to Paige confirming she'll be there as well, then I hop in the shower. As I soap up, my mind drifts to Paige. She's made her way under my skin, into parts of me I didn't know existed. She surprises me, intrigues me, and leaves me wanting more every time. She might seem like a quiet bookworm, but underneath the prim and proper speech patterns and the subdued clothing is a passionate woman who needed to be set free. And I'm more than willing to be the guy to help her do just that.

I'm the first to get to the bar, so I go ahead and order a few pitchers from Dean and take over a large table. Ethan and Summer are the next ones to show up, and Finn and Ashley arrive soon after. We're all hanging out, having a beer, when Summer moves beside me.

"Not to be super pushy or anything, but have you given any thought to my offer? I would love to figure out the details for the upcoming summer season if we could plan something."

Right. That.

Part of me wants desperately to take her offer and run with it. Make my dream come true and be done with the stifling responsibilities I've carried the last few years.

The truth is, it was easy to take on the story of wanting to start my own outdoor tour company back in the beginning, when I didn't want Paige to know who I really was and what I was doing in town. I'd held on to that dream for so much of my life, sharing it with people felt natural.

But it was also easy to forget. One phone call with my dad, and my head is right back in the family business, thinking of the next task I have to do. I may not enjoy my job, it may not be what I want to be doing with my life, but I'm good at it, and I'll damn well do my best to make my family proud.

"Summer, the truth is, I don't know what my plans are after next week. I have some upcoming commitments on the mainland I need to deal with, so I'm not exactly certain when I'll be back." Even though it isn't a complete lie, I feel like shit. Every time I'm reminded of the fact that these people don't know who I really am, it sucks. They're good people. Friendly. The kind of people I would want to hang out with if I was Wyatt James, not Wyatt James *Crawford*.

A sound of dismay has me spinning around in my chair. If I thought Summer was disappointed by my answer, it's nothing compared to the look on Paige's face.

"You're leaving in less than two weeks?" she asks in a small voice that sends a dagger to my heart.

Well, shit. Suddenly my clear head isn't so clear anymore.

Chapter Eighteen

Paige

"I.... Yeah, I have to go back to deal with some things. I was going to tell you tonight."

At least he seems remorseful, but that doesn't lessen the sharp pain I felt at hearing him tell Summer he was leaving so soon.

The rational side of my brain knew this day would come. It's why I wanted to initiate the conversation with Wyatt about our relationship far sooner. But my fear of rejection was stronger than my desire for knowledge, and now I am paying the price.

I nod stiffly, then pick up the glass of beer closest to me and take a long drink, making a face at the bitter taste.

"Want me to get you some wine instead?" Wyatt asks gently, and I give him a small smile of thanks.

He steps away, and Summer leans across his vacant seat. "Paige, I'm so sorry. I had no idea you didn't know he was planning to leave so soon. Are you okay?"

"I'm fine. I knew he was only here temporarily." I can't say anything more because Wyatt returns and sets a glass of white wine in front of me before sitting back down and draping his arm over my shoulders and leaning in.

"Are we okay?" he murmurs into my ear, his hand playing with my hair that I left loose for the evening. It feels so soothing and intimate, my head automatically leans into his touch.

"Yes. Of course." I keep my answer short because truthfully, I don't know what to say. Am I okay? In what definition of the word? Am I happy he is leaving? No. Do I acknowledge that it was inevitable? Yes. Does that make me okay? I am uncertain.

My mixed emotions are made all the worse by the headache I have been fighting off since lunchtime. Coupled with the dry scratchy feeling in my throat, I suspect I am coming down with a cold. Suddenly, a bar with all of my friends who are happy in their loving relationships is the last place I want to be. I want to be in bed, with a cup of hot tea, and Polly curled up beside me.

"I think I'm going to head home. I'm not feeling very well," I announce to the table, pushing my chair back. Wyatt stands up with me, his hand going to my lower back.

"Are you okay?" Summer asks, reaching her hand out to touch mine.

"Yes, I suspect my immune system is succumbing to a mild virus. That's all." I try to smile reassuringly, but given Summer's worried look, I suspect it comes out differently.

"I'll take you home." Wyatt picks up my jacket and holds it open for me, and I slip it on gratefully. We say our goodbyes and make our way to the parking lot. I was able to get a ride with Serena, so when Wyatt leads me straight to his car and holds open the door for me, I go along easily. The entire drive to my house is filled with a heavy silence. Until, that is, we get to my house and pull into the driveway.

"The guys took me for a trail run today," Wyatt says as we walk up to my front door.

This seemingly random comment takes me by surprise. Uncertain of how to respond, I simply say, "Oh."

"Yeah, I guess Mila told Ethan and Jackson that I was important to you, and they needed to make an effort to get to know me."

My hands freeze as mortification floods my veins. In light of what he just revealed regarding his plans to leave, this is even more inappropriate for my friends to do. "That must have been awkward. Wyatt, I am so very sorry for her interference. She had no right to push them into forcing a relationship with you."

Wyatt's hands cover mine, and he unlocks the door and ushers me inside. "It wasn't awkward, Paige. It was fun. Your friends are great people."

"Still, they should not be implying our relationship is something it is not." I go to the kitchen and let Polly out of her crate, picking her up and hugging her wriggling body into my chest. Her small tongue licks my chin enthusiastically, providing an affectionate and loving touch I need right now. Even if I wish it were Wyatt providing that affection instead of a dog.

"What does that mean?"

I hear Wyatt pull out a chair behind me. Putting Polly down on the floor, I go to the stove and fill the kettle with water before facing him. When I do, he's holding Polly, letting her cover his face in loving licks just as she did mine.

"I'm not sure what you're asking, Wyatt. We aren't in a defined relationship, are we? I realize we have never had a conversation about this, but the fact that you are only here temporarily has not escaped my attention."

"Fuck. Paige," Wyatt starts, then sets down Polly before standing up and walking over to me. One hand goes to my chin, the other my hip. He tilts my head up, forcing me to look into his eyes. "You're right, we never defined anything. But be honest. What's going on here, it's.... Well, it's something, isn't it?" He leans in, and I see his Adam's apple bob up and down as he swallows. Something inside me flutters in response to his apparent hopefulness. He's going to kiss me, and I don't think I could withstand that right now while I am in such turmoil.

I turn away, thankful for the whistle of the kettle pulling my attention from him. "Yes. It's something," I say, avoiding looking at him. I lift the kettle off the heat, but before I can do anything else, Wyatt comes beside me and reaches to grab two mugs. The fact that he is familiar enough in my home to know where I keep mugs is such a small thing, but it hits me with a heavy thud straight to my heart. I go to another cupboard and take out the honey and set it beside the mugs.

"Why don't you let me do this." Wyatt's hands come to my shoulders, and he steers me out of the kitchen. "You go and run a hot bath, I'll make your tea and get you settled."

He's being so kind. So thoughtful. I twist under his hands, ready to protest, to say I'm not that unwell, even though the truth is, my headache is getting worse and my throat now feels like I am swallowing razor blades. Wyatt must sense my resistance because he pushes my shoulders more firmly.

"Go, baby. I can see you don't feel great. Let me take care of you, please?"

His obvious desire to care for me, combined with the hopeful expression when he said he thinks there is something between us, is my undoing. The protective layer around my heart unravels as I feel my thoughts and dreams reconfigure into something new. Something not yet defined but includes Wyatt as a tangible part of my future. The uncertainty of it all is unnerving to say the least, but I don't have the mental or physical capacity to analyze it any further today.

Instead, I do as he tells me and go to the bathroom. A soak in a hot bath does sound nice. I add some rose scented bath salts and light a candle on the counter. When the tub is full, I take off my clothes and climb in, sinking down in the warm water and closing my eyes. I hear Wyatt move into my bedroom, but I can't quite determine what he's doing. But only a few moments pass before he comes into the bathroom, his shirt gone, and he sinks to the floor beside the tub. He places a glass of water within reach.

"Your tea is on that electric mug warmer thing, waiting by your bed. I figured a cool drink might be nicer right now."

His thoughtfulness touches me. But it's the sight of him, barefoot and shirtless, in my candlelit bathroom that has me filled with yearning. More than physical, I want all of him. I want his heart.

"Thank you," I say quietly. As I shift in the water, the sound of it sloshing against the tub draws his gaze away from my face. His eyes travel the length of my body, naked under the water, and I feel myself respond under the scrutiny. My nipples pebble and my legs draw together. Even though I am most assuredly unwell, I can no more deny my physical attraction to Wyatt than I could deny my emotional feelings for him. Feelings that are growing dangerously strong in light of his eventual departure.

The air around us crackles with something indescribable. Heat and arousal is evident in Wyatt's eyes, but as soon as he meets my gaze, he abruptly stands. "I'll leave you to it." He turns as if to leave, but I'm not ready for him to go.

"Wait. You could...join me?"

A slight frown furrows his brow. "Paige, you're sick."

"I know. You're right. Sorry. Thank you for the tea." I close my eyes and sink down in the tub, wishing it could wash away my embarrassment. Of course he wouldn't want to join me in the bath while I am unwell. There is no sexual appeal to my current state.

Hands come to my shoulders, gently pushing me forward. How he removed his clothes so quickly baffles me, but there is no mistaking his nudity as Wyatt climbs into the tub behind me. "Move up, baby."

I shift forward, and his legs come around the outside of mine, then Wyatt tugs me backward until I'm reclined against his chest. His arms settle around me, scooping warm water and letting it run over my skin. His lips press to the top of my head.

"Didn't I tell you I love hearing you ask for what you want?"

"Yes, but —"

"No buts, baby. Don't misunderstand me, I don't want to leave. I just know you aren't feeling well, and I wanted to give you some space."

"You make me feel better." The confession pours out of me before I can stop it or think about how he may receive a statement like that. But I feel his lips curl up in a smile against the top of my head, and then his hand gently tips my chin up so he can reach my lips where he kisses me again. I try to pull back, making a noise of protest, but Wyatt is stronger, and holds me there for one more press of his lips.

"You'll get sick, Wyatt."

"I don't care. You need to know I care about you, and I want to be here for you."

Speechless, I can't do anything except twist more fully so I can look at him, the steam making his hair around his face curl. I trace a droplet of water down his chest and lay my hand flat over where his heart beats strongly. Then, I take a deep breath, and for the first time in years, I let go and enjoy the sensation of being cared for.

Eventually, the water cools and Wyatt opens the drain with his foot before climbing out of the tub and grabbing two towels.

He quickly ties one around his waist, then wraps me up in the other, rubbing his hands all over my body gently. The soft smile on his face is warm, caring, affectionate, and fills me with hope that perhaps my growing feelings are not one-sided. I know he said he feels there is something between us, and when I am not fighting off a cold, I resolve to ask him what he means by that. But for now, my head is pounding and I am exhausted. I let Wyatt steer me into the bedroom where he picks up his T-shirt and pulls it over my head. It smells like him and barely covers my torso. Wyatt leads me back into the bathroom, prepares my toothbrush, and sets a bottle of pain relievers beside me before leaving me with a wink.

"I'll meet you in bed, baby."

As I brush my teeth, realization hits me. He's enjoying this.

Doting on me, even in small ways, like putting toothpaste on a toothbrush, is perhaps his way of demonstrating his feelings for me.

And that is enough for now.

When I'm finished, I open the door to the bedroom to see Wyatt standing beside the bed wearing nothing but his underwear. The duvet is drawn back, my tea still has a tendril of steam rising from it, and several candles are lit around the room. Exhaustion is hitting me, and all I care about is sleep. I walk past him, giving him a tired smile, and climb into bed, pushing the button to turn off the mug warmer underneath my tea.

"I think I'm too tired for that," I say in response to his questioning glance. Wyatt nods, then pulls the duvet up, kisses my forehead, and straightens.

"I'm just going to get Polly settled, I'll be right back."

A few minutes later, he shuts off the light in the bathroom, walks around to the other side of my bed before climbing in, and opens his arms to me. I move over and lay my head on his chest as his arms come around me.

"Thank you," I whisper as my eyes start to droop instantly. The last thing I hear — and to be fair, I'm half asleep, so perhaps I misheard — are three whispered words that go straight to my heart.

"Anything for you."

If only *anything* could include him staying with me.

Chapter Nineteen

Wyatt

Leaving Paige this morning was torture. Despite sleeping fairly soundly in my arms, her cold clearly worsened overnight. When she eventually woke up, her nose was congested, her voice half gone, and her head was still aching. I wanted to stay, but she begged me to go to the store and put up a sign telling her customers she wouldn't be open today. The only reason I agreed to leave was because she promised me that she was going to stay in bed and rest. A part of me knew I was overreacting and it was just a cold, but I also couldn't shake my worry for her.

After putting up a sign at the store, I send her a text to check in. The picture she sends in reply of Polly curled up on top of her legs, which are clearly covered by her duvet, reassures me enough that I decide to deal with a few other things before heading back over to her house. My first stop is the local grocery store where I grab some juice, fruit, and things to make sand-wiches. Easy food for me to prepare and for Paige to eat. When I pass by the small floral section, on a whim, I grab a bouquet of colourful flowers. I've never bought flowers for a woman before, but I'll do anything to bring a smile to Paige's face.

Back at my parents' house, I quickly shower, get dressed, and throw together a bag with a few changes of clothes. I'm not leaving Paige until she either kicks me out or she's better. If I get sick, so be it. Being by her side and caring for her is the only thing I can think of doing right now.

I go to pack my laptop, then hesitate. I don't want to risk Paige seeing anything associated with Crawford Books on my computer. I hate that I'm still lying to her. When she's better, I'll tell her. I have to. Instead, I quickly sit down at the counter to deal with any important emails before I go back over to her house. But as always happens, I get bogged down in work tasks for over an hour before I can finally close the laptop. Going to the door, I pull out a pair of shoes as my phone rings. I could ignore it, but a glance at the caller ID shows it's my father again.

"Two days in a row? Everything okay?" I say by way of greeting, my mind only half on the call. The other half is thinking of stopping at Camille's, Mila's café, to pick up some soup and maybe some muffins for Paige.

"Yes, everything is fine. In fact, I wanted to let you know that your instincts were right. Rosemary got to Calgary last night, and she's already met with the broker and pushed through the purchase on the new location. You'd better watch your back, or that woman will be coming for your job title." Dad laughs, but I don't join in. Little does he know that would be a dream come true.

"Okay, great. Anything else?" I say hurriedly, trying to slide my other shoe on with one hand.

"Ah, one more thing. With Calgary underway, I wanted to quickly get your opinion on branching out further on the East Coast. There's interest from the Toronto team about adding a second location, but we don't have a management presence back east at all. It would require relocation for the better part of a year, I suspect."

A year. On the other side of the country.

A month ago, I would have jumped at the chance. Anything for a new challenge. But now, the idea of an entire country separating Paige and I isn't so appealing, and I find that I'm not as quick to say yes. Dad must sense my hesitation.

"Is everything alright, son?"

Keeping my shoes on, I let out a loud sigh and lean back against the wall. "Yeah, Dad. I just...I don't know if I want to be on the East Coast for a year."

"Why? I thought you enjoyed your time in Toronto earlier. Oh, hang on, your mother just walked in. Let me put you on speaker phone."

Great. My mom is even more intuitive than my dad. Now I have no choice but to come clean.

"Hi honey." My mom's voice comes through the phone.

"Hey, Mom."

"So you were saying," Dad chimes in. "You're hesitant to go to Ontario. May we ask why?"

I think for a minute before responding, "Are you asking as my parents, or as my CEO and COO?"

"We're always your parents first, Wyatt," Mom says gently, and I let out my breath.

"Okay, then, the truth is, I'd like to stay on the West Coast for a while. I'll handle everything I can remotely, and only travel when I need to. I don't mind coming back for meetings in Vancouver, but...I was hoping to stay in Dogwood Cove. I...I met someone here."

My mother's gasp of excitement makes me smile. I think she'd like Paige. A lot.

"Okay, honey, we'll see what we can do to move things around."

"Giselle, you can't promise him that," my dad starts to protest, then I hear a muffled *ouch*.

"Mom, don't beat him up. He's right. I know you can't guarantee I can stay on this side of the country, I have a job to do. I just wanted to let you know where I'm at."

"Wyatt, I'm thrilled for you. And I can't wait to meet her. Maybe your father and I can come back to the island next week?"

I wince at how hopeful she sounds. But the truth is, I'm not sure I'll even want to be around Paige next week, especially on one particular day, much less Paige *and* my parents. "Maybe we could hold off for a little bit, Mom. It's still new."

"Fine, fine, I get it, you don't want your parents cramping your style."

It's so good to hear Mom joking like this, I smile into my phone. "Thanks, Mom."

"Look, Wyatt." My Dad's voice comes back on the phone. "If you'll agree to at least go to Toronto periodically, I think we can shuffle things around so you can stay here for the most part. Okay?"

God, I almost wish they weren't so accommodating sometimes. It would make me feel a lot less guilty about wanting to walk away from the company, and away from my job, if my parents didn't make it so easy to work for them. But this right here is exactly why I can't ever tell them I'm unhappy.

"Thanks, Dad. Listen, I gotta go. We'll talk soon, okay?"

When I finally get off the phone, I stand up, shoes untied, but on. I need to go to Paige. I need to tell her I'm staying, and that I want to give this thing between us a real shot. I want...well, fuck. I want her. In my life.

I'm smiling the entire drive to Camille's café, as I place my order at the counter, and as I walk next door to the bakery. Mila's behind the counter and puts her hands on her hips, looking at me skeptically.

"Why are you so damn happy?"

I shrug and just keep smiling. "Just am. Hey, what's Paige's favourite thing to get here?"

"Oh *that's* why you're happy." Mila waggles her eyebrows and I just laugh. She's not wrong.

She gets to work filling a bag with various things before handing it over to me. "Is she feeling better?"

"It's just a cold," I say confidently, but Mila frowns.

"She has to be careful, even with colds. It can turn bad quickly with her lungs."

I fight back the fear that ignites in me. Paige is fine. I left her just a couple of hours ago. "I'll take care of her, don't worry."

Someone in the kitchen calls Mila's name, and she turns to go. "You're good for her, Wyatt, just don't hurt her. Or I'll hurt you."

"Understood."

When I finally get back to Paige's house, I unload everything and put it by her front door before pulling out the key she gave me this morning so that I could lock up when I left. Opening the door, I listen to hear if she's awake, but the house is silent. She and Polly must still be asleep upstairs. I head into the kitchen to put away the food, but I come to a stop when I see Polly lying down inside her crate. She lifts her head with a soft whine.

Frowning, I crouch down and open the door, scooping the puppy out. "What are you doing locked up? Were you bugging Paige? She needs to rest, you silly thing." A lick to my chin is all I get in response. Tucking her under my arm, I head down the hallway to check on Paige.

When I see her bed empty, my confusion grows. Putting Polly down, I pull out my phone and dial Paige's number.

"Wyatt?" A woman answers, but not the one I was expecting.

"Serena? Why do you have Paige's phone?"

"Oh boy, umm, Wyatt, we're at the hospital. Paige's lungs started to seize up on her."

My phone falls to the ground. I squeeze my eyes shut as if that will push away the ringing in my ears. Panic. This is panic. Serena's small voice somehow reaches me and I swiftly bend and pick up the phone.

"Is she okay?" I bark out, searching the room for Polly. I scoop up the dog and jog back to the kitchen. Now I know why she was locked up. Grabbing my keys, I'm out the door as I take in Serena saying that Paige is being treated by the doctors, but they won't tell her anything else.

"I'm on my way."

It's a fucking miracle I don't crash my car on the drive to Westport. As it is, I make it in well under the time it should have taken. I park crookedly in the nearest stall I can find and race in the front entrance doors, my eyes searching frantically for Serena. When I find her, she's pacing back and forth in front of some empty chairs.

"What happened? Why is she here? Why did she call you? Is she going to be okay? What have they said?" Questions are pouring from me and distantly, I realize I sound like a crazed asshole, but I don't care. Serena's eyes are watery, and that only adds to my panic.

"Slow down, Wyatt, you're freaking me out."

I force a slow breath in and out, fisting my hands at my sides. "Serena, please."

"I'm her emergency contact. She's got her phone programmed to call me if she pushes a certain button. We set it up when she was having a hard time controlling her asthma, but she hasn't had to use it in years. I got her here as fast as I could, and they took her straight to the back. But they haven't come out to tell me how she is."

"Fuck." I sink down in a hard plastic chair as the adrenaline that got me here so quickly, abruptly drops off, leaving nothing but a deep fear in its place. I'm dimly aware of Serena sitting down beside me, tapping something on her phone.

What feels like forever passes before a woman wearing scrubs comes over to us.

"Are you the ones who brought Paige Millstone in?" We both shoot to our feet.

"Yes, I did, I'm her emergency contact, Serena. Is she okay? Did you give her nebulizers? She's latex sensitive, the nurses remembered that, right?" I put my hand on Serena's arm to stop her endless ramble and she quiets.

"Please, how is she?" I ask, forcing my voice to remain steady.

"She's stable, but weak. Her airway was quite inflamed, and her breathing rate was a lot higher than we like to see. I think we'll keep her overnight so we can provide a steady dose of steroids through the nebulizer, and as long as she maintains adequate oxygen saturation, she can go home in the morning."

I only absorb half of what the doctor says, but based on Serena's relieved "thank God" I'm guessing this is good news. It doesn't sound like it to me, but it's hard to really tell with all the chaos in my head.

"Can we see her?"

I look up when Serena asks the question, and when the doctor nods, I'm frozen. Torn between desperately wanting to see Paige and abject fear at seeing Paige in the hospital. But I force my feet to move and follow them into the back of the emergency department. Serena speeds up and sits down next to a stretcher. I walk a little closer, but stay back and let Serena have a minute first. I need the space to somehow get myself under control.

My eyes sweep over Paige, taking her in, cataloging everything. She's so pale and seems so small lying there on the bed, her long hair spread messily over the pillow, oxygen cannulas coming out of her nose, and a monitor clipped on to her finger. I watch Serena say something. Paige's eyes dart over to where I'm standing, and a tremulous smile comes across her beautiful face. I can't bring myself to smile back.

Yes, I've seen her in the ER before. But back then, I didn't know her. I didn't love her then.

But this is different. Because I do — love her, that is.

Which is why I can't do this. I can't be here. I can't watch another person I love suffer.

My hands tremble as I pull out my phone and open a text message to my father.

WYATT: Dad, I'll be in the office tomorrow. We can discuss me moving to Toronto after the 8th. I've changed my mind about staying here.

Chapter Twenty

I despise hospitals with ever fiber of my being. It's not the people that work there, oh no, I have the utmost respect and appreciation for every doctor, nurse, social worker, respiratory therapist, even the cleaning staff are inspiring in their dedication to their jobs and the patients they care for.

But when you spend most of your childhood in and out of hospitals, and your adult years doing everything possible to avoid more visits, it becomes very tiresome when your body simply lets you down.

The only way I was able to convince the doctors to let me go home and not admit me to the hospital was with Serena promising I wouldn't be left alone for at least the next week. I kept waiting for Wyatt to return, to tell Serena and the doctors that he would take care of me, but he never did. Just as he didn't answer my call when Serena drove me home, nor my text message later on last night.

It is all very confusing to me. Serena said he had seemed terrified for my well-being and desperate to see me when he first arrived at the ER. Why then, did he take off without even saying a word?

When I woke up this morning, alone in my bed after a fitful night of coughing and poor sleep, I roll over and hug his pillow to my chest. It smells like him. I can hear someone walking around in my kitchen and for a brief moment my heart leaps. Then I hear Serena talking to Polly. My confusion over his silence last night has morphed into hurt and embarrassment. I don't fully understand what happened, but I have apparently been deemed not good enough in some way. Not worthy of his attention anymore. Only this time, the pain is extra powerful as I realize I have been falling in love with Wyatt, and he clearly does not feel the same way.

I slowly move to a sitting position, wincing at the ache in my chest from a night of coughing. The fatigue will take a few days to pass as it always does when I'm battling a bad virus. At least this time the doctors are hopeful it won't settle into a pneumonia, thanks to the prophylactic antibiotics and steroids they sent home with me.

The door to my bedroom opens slowly, and Polly runs in with an excited yip, standing on her back legs at the side of the bed. Serena comes in and puts a tray down on the bed before lifting Polly up.

"How are you feeling?"

"Not well," I answer honestly.

"Physically, emotionally, or both?"

There are moments when Serena is so astute and so insightful into my own thoughts and emotions, it astounds me. With just that one question, she releases the chains that were holding back my hurt feelings. Tears start to roll down my cheeks, unrestrained.

"Oh Paige, I'm sorry." Serena passes over a tissue, and I wipe my eyes before blowing my nose in an extremely inelegant fashion. A bottle of hand sanitizer is passed to me next, and I take some, giving my best friend a watery smile.

"Thanks. I don't know why I'm crying." My voice trembles slightly.

"Well, I do. You spent the day in the hospital, your body feels like crap from fighting a cold and dealing with an asthma attack, and the guy who's meant to be here caring for you has ghosted you, leaving you stuck with me to play nurse. You're allowed to cry."

"Thanks, Serena," I whisper, sniffling into another tissue. "And you're a great nurse."

"I got you, babe. Always."

Serena squeezes my leg gently, offering a smile that is both sympathetic and filled with so much love.

One thing is for certain. I may not have Wyatt right now, but I do have my friends. And for that, I am so thankful. Because even if romantic love is not in my future, at least I will always have them.

Closing Pages for several days unexpectedly, like I had to do this week, was a hit to my bottom line. My budget can handle it, but not for much longer. Which is why, despite Serena's protests, I opened the store today, just three days after my visit to the emergency room. A large portion of my income is generated from online sales, and I have a lot of orders to package. Over the course of a few hours in the morning, I manage to take care of those, help a few customers, and book two space rentals for poetry readings.

When the bell above the door rings just as I'm preparing to close early, I can't hold back a sigh of dismay. But I paste on a smile and look up from my register book to greet my customers. But words escape me when I see Giselle Crawford, COO of Crawford Books, standing in my small independent bookstore, looking around nervously.

"Hello, may I assist you with something?" I close the logbook on the counter and fold my hands together in front of me, swallowing down my nerves. I have no clue what she is doing here, but it can't be a good thing.

"Oh yes, are you Paige, by chance?"

My eyes widen. How on earth does she know my name? "Y-yes," I stammer out.

"Would you happen to know where my son is?"

"Excuse me?"

"I'm sorry, dear, how rude of me. I'm looking for Wyatt Crawford, my son. The young man next door — Sebastian, I believe was his name — he told me you may know where I can find him."

My mind must still be addled from the medications I'm on because I believe I just heard her say Wyatt Crawford. But that can't be right, because the only Wyatt I know is Wyatt James. I feel as if I'm fighting against an invisible force, something holding me back from the truth.

Denial.

That must be what it is. My mind is refusing to acknowledge the possibility that Wyatt lied to me about his identity. Then again, he was always evasive with questions about his work, and his agitated behaviour and business attire at the Crawford Bookstore opening now makes a lot more sense.

"You must forgive my confusion," I say, quietly mustering the strength to confirm what I already know must be true. "The man I am familiar with went by the name Wyatt James. Is it possible that is who you're looking for?"

The surprise on her face disappears as quickly as it appeared. "Yes. That would be him. I apologize if he misled you, I cannot begin to understand why he would do that. Wyatt James *Crawford* is my son. He was here for a vacation in between launching new locations of our bookstores. And I'm hoping you can help me get in touch with him."

I nod slowly, letting everything sink in. But as I prepare to answer, to tell her I haven't seen her son — the man I thought

I knew — for several days, the door to my shop opens yet again and none other than Hank Crawford is holding the door open with one hand, a tray of drinks in the other, and Mila is hurrying in ahead of him with her flour covered apron on.

"Paige? These people say they're Wyatt's parents. Is he okay? Are you okay?"

My friend hurries over to me, examining me, as if looking for a physical mark. But the pain isn't on the outside of my body. It's inside. On my heart.

"That is correct, Mila. This is Hank and Giselle Crawford, of Crawford Books. Wyatt is their son. Apparently, he works for their company and was here on vacation."

My voice comes out far stronger and with more clarity than I am currently feeling.

"What the actual fuck?" Mila's outburst has all the shock and betrayal that I want to convey, so I stay silent as she puts her hands on her hips and glares at Wyatt's parents. "Can you please explain why he told all of us his name was Wyatt James and he was here to research opening an outdoor adventure tourism company?"

Hank and Giselle share a look, Giselle's eyes filling with tears. A part of me wants to go to her, to tell her it isn't her fault. Her love for Wyatt is evident, as is her pain. Hank wraps an arm around her shoulders, holding her briefly before answering.

"I'm sorry, ladies. I wish we could explain Wyatt's actions, but we can't just yet. Perhaps after we speak to our son, we can all gain some understanding of the situation."

"Unfortunately," I say quietly, my eyes downcast, "I have no idea where he is."

There's no mistaking Giselle's dismay at that. "Oh Hank, I knew he would do this again. We should never have tried to force him to be with us tomorrow. He's probably halfway to St. Thomas by now."

"What's happening tomorrow and what's in St. Thomas?" Once again, Mila comes to my rescue, asking the questions I so desperately want answers to.

Giselle lifts her tear-streaked face up to look me square in the eye. "Tomorrow is the anniversary of Wyatt's twin brother's death."

"And St. Thomas? Is that where his wife is? I mean, come on, what other secrets and lies is this guy hiding?"

"Mila," I say sharply. "That's not necessary." Mila huffs and folds her arms over her chest, and continues to glare at Hank and Giselle, as if it is all their fault.

"I assure you, my son is not married. He, well, he spoke of you, Paige. The last time we talked." Hank looks at me with a sad smile. "He said he wanted to stay in Dogwood Cove because of a woman. I assume he meant you."

I stumble backward as if his words are a physical blow.

"St. Thomas is nothing more than the location of a resort Wyatt and his friend Jacob have visited in the past. The Indigo Royal Resort. Jacob is down there and invited Wyatt to join him."

Mila and Wyatt's parents carry on talking, but the conversation fades to a buzz around me as I find a stool behind the counter and sink onto it. All this talk of resorts, and anniversaries, and who knows what else is confusing and simply too much to process.

"None of this matters; the bottom line is that Wyatt disappeared several days ago when I was in the ER with an asthma attack. I haven't seen or heard from him since."

Hank and Giselle share another look, this one with far more understanding.

"Paige, I'm not certain how much Wyatt shared with you about his brother Ryder. But ever since we lost Ryder, Wyatt has struggled greatly to cope anytime someone he knows is sick or injured. Hospitals are his least favourite place to be, and if you, a woman he clearly cares about deeply, were hospitalized, I am not surprised that he handled it poorly."

"If by 'poorly' you mean disappeared without even checking to see if she's okay, and then ignoring every single attempt by Paige and the rest of us to get in touch with him? Then, yeah. He handled it poorly."

Mila's acerbic words surprise me. I suppose I didn't realize my friends would also be hurt by Wyatt's disappearance. She shrugs her shoulders at my curious look. "What? We all liked the guy. He was good for you, and he was good here."

"Ladies, please excuse us, we should go and see if Wyatt has returned to the house. I suppose if he isn't there, we'll return to the mainland."

I incline my head in acknowledgment of Hank's words. But as they go, Giselle stops and pivots back to face us. I don't want to see the hope written in her expression, but I do.

"If my son is wise enough to realize his mistake and come back to you, I do hope you'll hear him out. Wyatt has so much love to give, and whether it's a mother's intuition or something else, I can see that you are who he needs — this town is what he needs — to properly heal at last."

I have absolutely no idea how to respond to her. Instead, all I do is nod slowly. She gives me one last smile. "And your store is absolutely lovely."

As the door closes behind them, Mila mutters, "What in the actual fuck."

"My thoughts exactly."

Chapter Twenty-One

Wyatt

"Twelve years, brother. Twelve fucking years."

I take another drink of Jack straight from the flask, ironically, one of an engraved set given to Ryder and I on our twenty-first birthday, my eyes staring out over the grey waters of English Bay. The beach is empty, no one else is stupid enough to be outside in this cold drizzle.

I've spent this day alone for the last twelve years. It seems appropriate, seeing as I left Ryder to die alone. A small penance, but one I must bear.

"Things were going good for awhile this year. The company is fine, Mom and Dad are fine. I bought a new car, a Tesla. Figured you'd get a kick out of me being environmentally conscious." A sad laugh escapes me, thinking of how often Ryder and I butted heads on issues like carbon footprint. It was one of those dumb brother arguments, seeing as I was just as concerned about those types of things as he was, but with him being the brainiac of us, it was fun to rile him up in a debate. "We opened three new locations, including another one over on the island. Westport. I stayed at the old summer house in Dogwood Cove. Man, that place has changed, and yet, seemed exactly the same as when we were kids. You would probably hate how chill and relaxed it was, but...I loved it."

Another swig of whiskey goes down, and I let the heat of it slide down my throat, reminding me that for better or worse, I'm still here. A seagull screeches over my head, the only sound other than the never-ending traffic noise behind me, and the waves hitting the shore in front of me.

"Do you ever wonder where we would be if you were still alive? I sure as shit wouldn't be sitting on a beach in the rain like some bum, drinking Jack out of a paper bag." I let out a harsh laugh and take another drink. "You'd be on your way to taking over the company. Dad would be gearing up to retire. I'd be, ah, who the fuck knows. Probably on a different beach, hopefully not drunk and alone." My head drops down with the weight of everything. "Guess it doesn't matter anyway," I mumble under my breath. Nothing matters right now.

My phone vibrates in my pocket. Damnit, I thought I left it in the car. There's no point in looking to see who it is, the only people still trying to reach me are my parents. And I don't want to talk to them. They know I'm okay, I did tell them that. But I didn't say where I was or what I was doing. The last thing I need is them showing up. I doubt anyone else would be trying to reach me today. Everyone at work knows what November 8th is in our family, and they leave us alone. As for everyone in

Dogwood Cove? Those calls and messages stopped yesterday. I guess everyone finally gave up. The first two days after I left, Paige tried to reach me several times. Aside from reading the one that said she was home from the hospital, I've deleted them all. Then Serena, Summer, and even Finn started trying to contact me. I'd say I was touched that they all care enough to reach out, but the truth is, it just made me angry. At myself, not them.

How the hell did I let myself get so close to them? Close enough that they apparently miss me, and I miss them. I miss the life I fooled myself into believing I was living in Dogwood Cove.

I miss Paige.

"You would've liked her, Ry. She's quirky, fucking genius-level smart, curious, kind, insightful — damn, she reads me like a book. Just like you used to. I know you'd tell me to pull my head outta my ass and go and apologize, but I can't. I can't keep her, only to lose her. You don't know." My voice breaks as I choke on a cry. "You don't know how hard it was to lose you. You were the other half of me, and I lost you. I can't lose her the same way."

The drizzling rain turns heavier, and in minutes, my face is wet with more than just the evidence of my grief.

"I screwed everything up, brother. And now there's no way out. I wish you were here to tell me how to fix this, fix me. Because I've been broken ever since you left. And the one chance I had to maybe change that, I threw it away because I'm so fucking scared of breaking even more."

Saying the truth out loud, admitting it to myself and to Ryder should feel like a release of some sort, shouldn't it? I've never acknowledged it so fully before. But it doesn't. It feels hollow — too little, too late. It doesn't take a genius to recognize I walked away from Paige out of fear, just like it doesn't take a genius to know I'm being a cowardly fool by letting that fear rule my life. But just like the guilt I let dictate my work life, this fear has assumed full control of my personal life. And it holds that control with a choke hold.

Time passes, as it always does. Eventually, my fingers are numb, and I can't stop shivering. Reluctantly, I stand, and looking straight out at the ocean, I lift the flask to the sky one last time.

"Cheers, Ry. I miss you."

After I take one long, final drink, I tuck the nearly empty flask in my coat pocket and head up the beach to the sidewalk that leads to my apartment. Tomorrow I'll head back to Dogwood Cove and pack up the things I left at the house before going to Toronto for a week or so to deal with things out there. After that, I have no clue what I'll do. Back to Vancouver, back to work, I suppose. Back to the life that was never meant to be mine.

It was a mistake to drive down Main Street. I knew it as soon as I turned off the highway. I should have taken the back roads to get to my parents' house. Get in, grab my stuff, get out. But for some fucked-up reason, I decided to torture myself with driving through the town center of Dogwood Cove and have my face rubbed in the life that could have been, if I was anyone but me.

The gazebo. What town has as fucking gazebo? Dogwood Cove does. And I can't lie, I pictured kissing Paige there. Cheesy as fuck, but I wanted to.

Sweet Scoops, the ice cream place Paige told me about a week or so ago. She said that in the summer, the lineup on Thursdays is around the block because the owner releases specialty flavours. Her favourite was a caramel pecan praline that sounded delicious.

The Nutty Muffin. The place I first laid eyes on Paige. I can't believe how quickly I dismissed her. To think, if I hadn't gone next door to her store, I never would have fallen in love with her.

Maybe then I wouldn't feel like such a pile of fucking shit. I keep my eyes forward as I drive past Pages. I don't want to see her. I can't see her.

When I finally pull into the driveway at the house, I sit in the car with my eyes closed for several minutes. I've made a mess of everything, there's no denying it. I'm living a life I fucking hate. And there's no way out.

All I can do is pack up, go home, and continue life as Wyatt Crawford, the twin who lived. The twin who has to do every fucking thing possible to live up to his brother. Fill the shoes that are impossible to fill.

Slowly, I climb out of the car and walk to the front door. Inside, I head to the bedroom and start throwing clothes into my suitcase haphazardly. I'm almost done when there's a knock at the door. No one knows I'm here, so I ignore it. But then I hear the door open, and the one voice I didn't want to hear calls my name.

"Wyatt? Please come and talk to me." She's trying to sound strong, but I hear the pain in every word. Knowing I caused that pain? Well, let's just say I feel it in my own heart tenfold.

Making my way out of the en suite, I try to mentally prepare myself for seeing her. But nothing can prevent the gut punch I feel at seeing Paige standing in front of me. So close, yet so fucking far. She's wearing leggings and an oversized sweater. Her hair is up in one of her messy buns, and she looks miserable, just as I'm sure I do. I stand frozen as she hugs her arms around her middle. The action makes her look small, vulnerable, and I want to pull her into my arms and protect her, build her up, tell her how strong she is.

But she isn't strong. Her body is frail. It could fail at any time.

I could lose her. And that's why I won't take another step. Better to push her away now, before we get any closer.

That's a fucking joke. I love her. Can't get much closer than that.

"Your parents were here looking for you."

Of all the things I thought she would say, that isn't even on the list. I rub my chin as I try to figure out what to say to her, but she beats me to it.

"They were worried about you. We all were. Especially when they told me about yesterday. Why didn't you tell me it was Ryder's anniversary? I would have been there for you."

The heartbreak in her voice goads me into action, and I head into the kitchen, grabbing my water bottle off the counter and then stomping into the living room to drop it into a bag I have on the couch. "I didn't *want* you there. I didn't want anyone." I continue my slow walk through the open space of the house, gathering the few things I had left around. Even though I refuse to look at her, I feel Paige. I feel her everywhere.

"Is that how you are choosing to live your life? Without anyone?"

Her question cuts me to the bone. She is the one person, aside from my brother, who could see through everything in an instant.

"It's better that way."

"Better for whom? Not for the people who care about you."

I shake my head. "You don't get it, Paige."

"You're right, I don't. Maybe before, I would have understood. Why open yourself up to pain if you don't have to? I might have questioned if it was worth it. But you changed that. You changed me. You showed me that love is worth it. You made me love you."

"Fuck. Don't say shit like that." I barely manage to hold back from yelling at her. "You don't mean it, you said yourself you're not meant for romantic love. So how could you possibly love me?"

My words have the desired effect, despite the complete lie that they are. Paige's gasp has me closing my eyes against the self-hatred I feel at causing her pain.

"You're right. I fell in love with a lie, didn't I? Why is that, Wyatt? I let you in. I showed you my true self and you, you lied about everything. Your name, why you were here, was any of what we had true?" She ends on a sob and it just about breaks me. I want to tell her that it was all true. Everything I said and felt was true, or at least I wanted it to be. But then my mind flashes to seeing her on that stretcher in the ER.

"You should go, Paige," I say woodenly. "There's nothing here for you." I turn my back and wait to hear the door slam behind her. But it doesn't.

"You're right. There's nothing here except a man who can't admit he's scared. A man who would rather live alone than allow someone to love him. A man who would rather live a lie than take any real risks."

My eyes close against the attack of her words. Every single one is the goddamn truth. But I am paralyzed by that truth.

Finally, the door closes and I'm alone again.

The way it should be.

The way it always will be.

Chapter Twenty-Two

Paige

After I leave Wyatt's house, I find myself at a complete loss as to what to do. When I saw him drive past Pages, my heart leapt. Foolishly, I believed he was here to explain everything, to ask for forgiveness. Those hopes were dashed as soon as he spoke.

Despite the agonizing pain I am currently experiencing, I do not believe Wyatt meant most of what he said. He lashed out from his own pain and pushed me away in a desperate attempt to protect himself.

After speaking with his parents, I understand his likely reason for leaving. Do I agree with it? Absolutely not. Asthma is not cancer. It is not a death sentence. Yes, mine has been uncontrolled as of late, but an adjustment in my regular medications should fix that.

What I still struggle to comprehend is the lies he told me. Why wasn't he simply honest about who he was and why he was in town? I'm not an idiot, I quickly pieced together that he must have been here for the opening of the Westmount store.

How foolish do I feel now, recalling seeing him at the store and the furtive glances he made around the room. He was looking to see if someone would reveal his true identity. All the times he avoided giving complete answers about himself, the lack of any concrete details of his plans, it all makes sense now. The question is, why?

That question has gone around in my head at least a hundred times in the past hour. I drove around town, eventually ending up at Oceanside Beachfront Resort. Summer has turned this place around, but with it being November, there are only a few of the cabins booked, judging by the vehicles I see parked outside. Opening my door, I step out into the cold, damp air. I get Polly out of the backseat, and after I clip on her leash, I set her down. She instantly starts sniffing around, exploring the area.

"Paige? Hey! What are you doing here?" Summer walks out of the office building, wrapping her coat around her body. She stoops down and gives Polly some attention before straightening and looking at me. "How are you?"

"Not good," I reply, swallowing against the tears that are, again, threatening to fall.

Summer tucks her arm in mine and pulls me toward the door she just came out of. "Okay. Let's make some tea."

A short while later, we're both seated on the small couch in Summer's office, sipping jasmine tea. This is why I ended up here. Of all my friends, Summer is, by far, the most calm and steady one. From the moment she returned to Dogwood Cove,

I knew I had a kindred spirit in seeking calm and quiet moments to process life.

"Wyatt came back to town today," I say, keeping my eyes fixated on the pale liquid in my mug. "Not to stay, just to get his things."

"Did he say anything about why he disappeared?"

I shake my head. We sip our tea in silence for a minute as I try to make sense of everything in my mind.

"I know he was scared by my getting sick. I can fully acknowledge how that event would be triggering for him, given his experience of losing his brother. But..."

"But you wish his feelings for you were strong enough to overcome his fear?"

"Precisely."

Somehow, I let Summer convince me to go back to her and Ethan's house where Mila, Serena, and Ashley were waiting. Abby had to stay at the farm with her daughter Layla, and the men of our group were conspicuous in their absence. I am familiar with what my friends intend for tonight. Whenever one of them reached a difficult point in their relationships, we came together to support them in whatever way they needed.

The problem is, I am unable to identify what it is that would make me feel better in this situation. I've never fallen in love, much less had my heart broken. The pain I am feeling is as unfamiliar to me as the sheer ecstasy of an orgasm once was.

"What if I never have an orgasm again," I blurt out, courtesy of the bottle of wine Mila has systematically emptied into my glass over the past hour and a half.

"You will. He unlocked the door, but now anyone can walk in," Serena slurs from her place next to me on the couch.

I glare at her over my glasses, which have slipped down my nose. "That allegory is disturbing."

Serena giggles, then snorts, sending all of us into fits of laughter.

"I believe we have consumed a sufficient amount of alcohol for the evening. Why is my pain not subsiding?" I ask morosely, peering into the bottom of my empty glass.

"Because heartache takes more than booze to heal." Ashley's wise words have the rest of my friends nodding in agreement. I look at them in turn, and despite the wine clouding my brain, I notice even Serena, who is presently unattached, nodding.

"I believe I was happier before I knew this feeling. Perhaps my avoidance of romantic intimacy was a smart act of self-preservation."

"But," Mila reasons, "Then you wouldn't know about orgasms. And orgasms are good."

Summer gets up from her chair and goes to the kitchen, returning with a bag of popcorn and another bottle. She makes the rounds, filling up our glasses, then drops back down to sit with the popcorn, only for Mila to reach over and take it from her.

"Here's the thing, Paige. Love hurts. It sucks, but it's true. Whether it's your first crush in high school or the love of your life, love hurts."

"Hurts even more when it's a little bit of both," Serena mumbles, and all our heads turn to her.

"Excuse me? Story time?" Mila asks, but Serena waves her off.

"Later. Tonight is Paige's night."

"I'm quite content to shift the attention away from myself," I remark, but Serena gives me a glare that would be far more intimidating were it not for the alcohol in my bloodstream making me indifferent to it.

"Nope. As the solitary single woman of our group, I demand that we focus on you and not me. I am not equipped to handle the pressure of all you lovey-dovey people right now."

"Fine, but we're coming back to this, lady."

I feel Mila shift her attention back to me, and I take great care not to meet her gaze.

"Paige, look. Wyatt was hot, and he was into you, but he isn't the only guy out there. When you're ready, you'll meet someone who's right for you."

Once more, alcohol fuels my blunt confession. "I think he is the only guy out there. He was right for me. For once, I felt like I truly belonged with him. I've never had that before. Never felt like *I* was the right person, in the right place, *with* the right person."

"Not even with us?" Serena asks in a small, hurt voice.

"I know how this sounds, but no. Not even with you. I care for each of you deeply. You are truly amazing friends that I feel lucky to have in my life. But I have always felt as if I am on the periphery, looking in at a group of inspiring, strong, beautiful women who go after what they want in life and don't hold back." I look to Serena first. "You bought the studio from Madame Elaine and turned it into something even more. You instill such confidence and strength in every student you teach, changing them for the better." My eyes travel to Summer. "You came back, not knowing what you would find, handled the loss of your father, and created a future for yourself. You've proven yourself to be a capable businesswoman, and an integral part of our community." Mila's chewing on her lower lip when I reach her. "And you, you took a dream you had with your mother and made it a reality, single-handed. You run two business, and even had the time and energy to organize a fundraiser for animals. And Ashley." I look at my newest friend. "I don't know you very well, but you belong here. And just like the others, you've created a life you should be proud of."

"Don't you dare skip over yourself, if you're handing out praise for chasing dreams."

I'm taken aback by the fire in Serena's voice. She folds her arms across her chest, narrowing her gaze at me.

"Who is it that walked away from an incredibly sheltered life because she knew there was more out there? Not any of us, that's for sure. Who took a small inheritance and turned it into a profitable, successful store? Who pulls all of us together each month for book club? Who do we go to when we need someone to help us see reason and logic? Who helps all of us stay calm when we start to freak out? Good grief, Paige, do you honestly not see how important you are to all of us? How we wouldn't be *us* without you? You belong to each and every one of us. You are *my* best friend, and if I have to pin you down and force you to hear me say that over and over again, I will."

Serena stops, then abruptly throws her arms around me, pulling me into an awkward embrace. My glasses are knocked askew, but I can't do anything about it as she squeezes me tightly.

"I love you, Paige. You hear me?" she mumbles into my shoulder.

"Yes, Serena. I hear you." I pat her back. "And I...I love you, too."

"You better love all of us, woman."

Serena and I break apart, and I look at my friends. "I do. Truly. And I apologize if what I said hurt anyone. I suppose I spent so much of my life on the outside, I didn't realize I was on the inside. If that makes sense."

"It totally does." Ashley reaches a hand over from where she's sitting and places it on my knee. "And for what it's worth, I think you're inspiring and strong and amazing and all those things you think we are. And if Wyatt can't see that and realize your asthma doesn't define you or hold you back, then maybe you're better off without him."

"What she said." Mila comes and squeezes onto the couch on the other side of me, leaning her head down on my shoulder. "You deserve nothing but the best from life, and from anyone who shares that life with you. I'm sorry Wyatt hurt you, but we'll get you through this. I promise."

"Thank you," I whisper, just loud enough for them all to hear me. "I am a lucky woman to have all of you."

Mila stands, walks over to her bag, and returns with a box. "I almost forgot, the orders from the passion party came in." She hands the box to me with a smile. "Which means, not only do you have us, but you also have a vibrator now. No man required."

I manage a wan smile. I know she is simply trying to bring some levity to the situation. But the sad truth is, I cannot go back to my previous way of living. I now know how it feels to be connected with someone on an intimate level. I cannot ever forget how complete that made me feel.

Just as I cannot shake the belief that without Wyatt, I will never feel that way again.

Chapter Twenty-Three

Wyatt

"Fuck, I hate Toronto," I gripe on the phone to Jacob as I push my way through the crowded airport to the check in counter. I'm exhausted and grumpy. And every little thing is pissing me off.

"That's funny, I remember a time where you thought you might move there permanently. What's changed?"

"Nothing. I just don't see the appeal of a city packed full of people anymore."

"Uh huh, let me guess. Small town life got to you, didn't it. What's her name?"

I mutter a curse under my breath as I dodge a couple of people standing in the middle of my path, staring at their phones. "It doesn't matter."

"Oh, I think it does, my friend. Because something's got you in a god-awful mood, and I'm guessing it's a woman."

"Can't I just be in a bad mood? Not all of us are freshly home from several weeks lazing around on a beach surrounded by sun, sand, and beautiful women."

"And whose fault is that?" Jacob fires back. "I told you to come and join me, but you decided to stay up there."

I finally make my way to the lineup for check in and come to a stop. "You know I had to deal with the store opening."

"Yeah, but after that? Why did you stay?"

I don't answer right away. Even though the answer is simple. *Paige.*

"Look, Wyatt, what are you doing with yourself?

"Well, right now, I'm waiting to get on a plane back to Vancouver, listening to my best friend go all philosophical on me."

"Be serious. What would Ryder think if he saw you right now?"

He'd be pissed. "Point taken. But what exactly am I meant to do?" I shuffle forward.

"You're meant to stop being such a goddamn martyr for once."

Jacob's words have the effect I'm sure he intended. My initial reaction is anger, but it's swiftly eclipsed by remorse.

"Look, man, I don't wanna be the asshole who gives you shit about your dead brother, but I'm gonna have to. You're living his life, not yours, and if he were here right now, he would tell you to stop being such a fucking idiot. It's not gonna bring him back, you know that. So why are you making yourself miserable all the goddamn time?"

It's not the first time Jacob has tried to say this to me, and in the past, I've always dismissed it. But that was before I had a taste of what my life could be.

The line moves forward, and I'm next, giving me the perfect excuse to end a conversation that is making me face up to things I don't know if I'm ready to deal with. "I gotta go, Jacob. I'll talk to you when I land. We'll grab drinks tomorrow or something."

"Will you at least think about what I said? Whoever she is, I bet she's worth it."

"You have no idea."

I used to like my apartment. The view over English Bay, the open floor plan, clean lines, and simplistic design. It was perfectly fine as a place to return at the end of a day. Now it feels cold and empty. It takes all of twenty minutes to unpack my bag from Toronto and toss a load of clothes into the laundry. Then I find myself at a loss.

If I were still in Dogwood Cove, I'd probably head out for a hike, or go over to Pages to visit Paige. Hell, maybe I'd be at her house cooking dinner or doing some other mundane, yet perfectly peaceful task. I never thought I would be one to enjoy domesticity, especially not with another person. But with Paige, I did.

As I heat up some leftovers, frozen who knows how long ago, my phone beeps with an incoming message.

MOM: Hi honey, welcome home. If you're up for it, join your father and I for dinner tonight? I'll make cannelloni.

On cue, my stomach rumbles. I haven't had a home cooked meal with my parents in months, and Mom knows I can't resist her cannelloni.

WYATT: Sounds good. Be there in an hour

The leftovers go into my fridge for tomorrow, and instead of eating, I head downstairs to my building's gym and pound out a few miles on the treadmill before going over to my parents' house. I need the endorphin rush to clear the post-travel fog. Hopefully, it'll also give me the energy to put on a good enough front with my parents so they don't see right through my bad mood the way Jacob did.

But when I walk in the front door of their house in Point Grey, one look at Mom's face is all I need to know she isn't going to go easy on me. I'm about to catch hell for avoiding her ever since coming back from Dogwood Cove. I didn't acknowledge her attempts to reach out on Ryder's anniversary, and when I had to go to the office to grab what I needed for Toronto, I was careful to avoid both her and Dad's office. Which means Mama Crawford is about to lay it on me.

"Wyatt. So nice to see you at last." Her hands are on her hips, and despite the calm look on her face, I can sense the hurt, worry, and disappointment brewing underneath.

"Hey, Mom. How are you?" I walk over and kiss her cheek before handing her a bottle of the La Lune Rouge Meritage we enjoyed when they were on the island.

"Oh, I'm fine. The real question is, how are you?"

With that cryptic remark, Mom turns and walks into the kitchen. I guess I'm expected to just follow her, so I do.

"Hi Dad, Toronto went well."

My father turns from the cabinet where he's pulling down wine glasses. "Great. Thanks for taking care of that."

Huh. Weird. Normally he would have a lot more questions for me, questions that would come across as thinly veiled critiques of my work. Gingerly, I sit down on one of the tall bar stools that line the kitchen counter as my father wordlessly opens the bottle of wine I brought, pours three glasses, and slides one to me after handing the other to my mother.

I take a sip of wine, savouring the rich flavour. Finn knows his shit when it comes to making wine, that's for damn sure.

"We went to Dogwood Cove to look for you. Your mother desperately wanted to be with you on the eighth."

The wine goes down the wrong way, courtesy of my shock at hearing my father actually reference the date of Ryder's death. Has he ever done that? I honestly can't remember. And it would seem there's not going to be any small talk tonight, we're getting straight into it. I clear my throat and shift on my seat. "Yeah, I heard. Sorry I wasn't there."

"Care to share where you were? Your friends seemed just as disappointed by your absence as we were."

I don't even try to hide my wince. "Who did you speak with?"

Mom comes and sits down on the stool beside me. "Paige. And another woman, Mila. But Paige seemed particularly upset by your leaving. She's who you were talking about before, isn't she? When you said you wanted to stay in Dogwood Cove for a while?"

There's no sense in lying now. "Yeah, she was."

"What happened, son?" I lift my eyes to meet my father's, and I'm stunned to see nothing but compassion.

But opening up to them is not that simple. I've forced down my personal feelings for too many years, keeping my focus on trying to be a good son, to try and make up for the fact that Ryder is gone.

"Why do you think something happened?" I say, half-heartedly trying to avoid the question.

"Because we aren't blind, or stupid, even if it has taken us this long to realize just how unhappy you really are." At Mom's sharp tone, my head twists around to look at her. She reaches her hand out to rest on my leg. "I'm so sorry, honey, we've wasted too many years looking the other way, believing you were content, when this entire time you've been hurting far more deeply than we realized."

My entire body slumps down as tension I've been carrying for years dissipates. I let out a strangled laugh, my head falling back so I'm staring at the ceiling. "All I wanted was for you guys to not worry about me. To try and make up for the fact that you lost one of your sons. Sounds impossible, now that I say it out loud."

"Wyatt James Crawford, you fool. We're your parents. Worrying is what we do best." My mom sniffs tearily as she stands up and pulls me into her arms. "Hug me, son. Not because we lost your brother, but because we still have you. And you are enough, just the way you are."

I let myself collapse into her embrace, feeling it infuse me with the love I've pushed away for too long. My dad's hand comes to my shoulder and squeezes gently, and his support flows through as well.

"I don't want to work for Crawford Books," I mumble into my mom's shoulder.

"What?" she asks, pulling back slightly. I take a deep breath. It's now or never. *I'm doing it, Ryder.*

"I don't want to work for Crawford Books. I never have. I did it because I knew you wanted the company to stay in the family, but I'm sorry, it's not for me. I just can't see myself working in an office for forty more years without going fucking insane."

"Language, please." My mom's reprimand is a gentle one, but clear.

"Wyatt, we've been in talks with your uncle for years about taking Crawford Books public. We knew you would never want to take over as CEO, so keeping it in the family didn't make sense. Why didn't you tell us how unhappy you were sooner?" Dad's gruff voice comes from behind me, and disengaging from

Mom, I turn around to face him. There's no sense in hiding from my guilt and shame anymore, I have nothing left to lose.

"Ryder died alone because he and I fought over what I should do after he died. He...he wanted me to promise I would do something that we had talked about, but I refused. I didn't want to do it without him."

"Is that the outdoor tour company?" Mom asks quietly, and I turn to her in surprise.

"How did you know?"

She smiles softly. "Mila. She demanded to know why you had lied about why you were in Dogwood Cove. Apparently you told them you were there to research opening an adventure tourism outfit."

"Sounds perfect for you, son, you always were happier outside."

I drop my head and stare at the floor. "Yeah. Ryder and I were going to convince you to open an office branch of Crawford Books on the island, so we could just buy out a building as an investment. He'd have an office upstairs, and on the main floor would be WR Tours. He never wanted to be more than a silent partner, but we always said we'd do it together. I knew he was dying and I didn't think...I couldn't...I didn't want to do it without him."

Fucking hell. I'm crying in front of my parents. I haven't done that since Ryder's funeral. I saw how grief-stricken they were that day, and I vowed not to make it worse by showing them my own pain. But I can't help it.

"Oh, honey. All your brother wanted, all we want, is for you to be happy. To *live* your life. Not try to live his."

Mom's words are so similar to Jacob's, they hammer the message home even harder.

"I know, Mom. I'm starting to understand that," I say quietly. "And I want you to know, I'm so sorry I wasn't here for you when you needed me. His anniversary was so fuc-damn hard for me, I lost sight of how hard it must have been for you. I lost a brother, you lost a son. Hell, you sort of lost two sons with how much of an asshole I've been about everything." I drag my eyes up to my mom's face and see tears streaming down her cheeks. "I'm so sorry. To both of you. I hope you can forgive me for being so selfish."

"Of course we can, Wyatt. We were all just trying to get through and make sense of things the best way we could. Your need for space each year was no less important than our desire to be around you. We love you, no matter what."

I fold Mom into my arms for another hug, this time letting the cathartic release of guilt and grief happen.

Eventually, we part, and we all sit there for a moment, until my Dad breaks the silence.

"Where does Paige fall into all of this?" he asks, innocently enough, not realizing how hard that is to answer.

"Nowhere, not anymore." Those two words are perhaps the most painful ones of the entire conversation.

"Well, that's a damn shame, son. She seemed like a wonderful woman."

"She was. Is. She's amazing."

"Then why aren't you with her?"

I don't answer. Because I know that when I do, my parents will tell me to stop being an idiot. And they'd be right. But the fear of losing her is so strong.

"She told us about her asthma. How you left when she was in the hospital. We'll get to how disappointed I am that you would abandon the woman you care about in her time of need later, but right now, we need to talk about fear."

Mom is using that voice. The one Ryder and I used to call her Mama Bear voice. It meant business, as in, *shape up boys or you're in trouble*. Memories of the two of us hustling to try and avoid trouble come to me unbidden, and my lips tip up slightly.

"What exactly are you afraid of, Wyatt?"

I answer honestly. There's no other option. "Losing her."

"Well good for you, you made your fear a reality. How does it feel?"

"Fucking awful."

"Language." Mom slaps my leg gently.

"Sorry, Mom, but it's true. It feels horrible. As if I left part of my soul in Dogwood Cove and I'll never get it back," I answer hoarsely.

"Love is a risk. There's always a chance of heartbreak and pain and loss. But think of it this way. Would you have been happier if Ryder had never lived? If you never had a twin brother? That way you would have never lost him — would that be preferable?"

"God, no!" I answer in horror. "Of course not. That's in-sane."

"Mmm hmm." Mom crosses her arms in front of her chest and stares at me, waiting for the second it clicks.

"Shit." I drop my head into my hands. "Sorry, Mom."

"I'll let it slide this time."

"I need to fix this." I lift my head and look from Mom to Dad. "How do I fix this?" But no sooner do I say that than the answer comes to me.

"I need to find a book."

CHAPTER TWENTY-FOUR

Paige

"Thank you," I say to Ethan and Reid as they maneuver the new couch into position at the back of my store.

"No problem. Do you need anything else moved around?" Ethan rubs his hands on his pants as he and Reid look around the space.

"No, this was it. You're sure you don't mind taking the old couch to the secondhand store?"

"Nope, it's fine."

"Thank you."

I lock the front door after they leave and go to turn on my Joni Mitchell. For several days after Wyatt left, I couldn't bring myself to turn it on. My ritual was forever changed by memories of dancing with Wyatt in the dark. But today I woke up and my heart didn't hurt quite as much. I made it through the day without thinking of him more than once or twice. And I did not feel my heart leap every single time my phone beeped with an incoming message, naïvely hoping it would be him. The fact is, the only contact I have had that is remotely tied to Wyatt was an email sent to my store account from none other than Giselle Crawford. It came through just two days ago and simply said Wyatt was in Vancouver, and she hoped to see me again sometime. I read and reread her short message so many times, it is burned into my memory. I cannot begin to understand why she reached out, especially to say she wishes to see me again. Whatever for? I refuse to allow my heart to consider any possible future with Wyatt and his family in it. That path is far too dangerous to go down.

As the words and music of "Big Yellow Taxi" float through the air, I let my eyes drift closed and my hips start to sway. The inner peace that I used to always feel this time of day infuses me; the spirit and energy of my grandmother bringing a true smile to my face.

The sound of a loud knock on the door startles me, breaking my solitude. I'm hidden down one of the aisles of bookshelves, and as I briefly contemplate ignoring whoever it is, they knock again and I hear *his* voice.

"Paige? Baby, I see the light on. If you're there, please let me in."

A battle instantly starts in my heart. I desperately want to run to the door and open it, let him back into my life and into my heart. But I am wary. The devastation his leaving caused me was not something I ever want to repeat, and if he left once because of my asthma, what is to stop him the next time I have a flare up?

Fast on the heels of that dilemma comes another. How do I know he's here to ask for forgiveness at all? One pet name does not an apology make.

Ultimately, my curiosity wins out, and I slowly emerge from my place behind the shelf and make my way to the door. His eyes light up, and a smile unlike any I have ever seen before from him covers his handsome face. My greedy heart soaks it up like a plant receiving water after a drought. I turn the lock and step back, letting him push the door open. I stand there, silently waiting, as he closes the door behind him. He keeps some distance between us, for which I am thankful, even though it is physically painful being this close to him. Such a strange phenomenon, feeling such a strong yearning for another human being. I have never *wanted* anyone like this before.

"Paige, I..." His hand comes up to rub his jaw as his eyes sweep up and down my body. "Fuck. Baby. I have so much I need to say, but it's just so good to see you."

I cross my arms in front of me stiffly. "I am not certain I can say the same for you just yet."

"I deserve that." Wyatt inhales audibly, letting it out on a sigh as his hand now moves up to run through his hair. "I am so sorry for leaving the way I did. For leaving at all. I don't have a fucking clue how to earn your forgiveness, but I'm hoping you'll at least hear me out on a few things. Please. I really need to explain."

This is it. The moment I decide if I am willing to open myself to him once more. But my body answers for me, before my heart and mind have a chance to catch up. Turning with a small tilt of my head for him to follow, I lead the way to the new couch Ethan and Reid set in place not too long ago. I sit at one end, angling my body to face him as he sits at the other end. The couch is small, so the distance between us could easily be bridged. But neither one of us reaches out for the other.

"I've had my parents and my best friend all tell me what a stupid coward I was. How wrong I was to walk out on you like that. And worst of all, how mad my brother would be at me, not only for leaving you, but for living my life the way I have since he died." Leaning forward, Wyatt drops his elbows to his knees and looks at the floor. His back is hunched with pain that I ache to soothe away. "Losing him broke me. And I thought I was doing the right thing by avoiding any sort of relationship that might lead to that kind of pain again. It was easy at first. For years, no one came into my life that made me think twice about getting involved. But you changed everything."

Finally, he looks at me, and I'm shocked to see tears glistening in his deep brown eyes. His hand comes up to brush them away.

"I've cried more this past week than I did when Ry died. If that doesn't tell you something, I don't know what will. Here's the thing. My mom made me see just how colossal of a mistake I made. She asked me one simple question. Would I have been happier if Ryder had never existed, so that I would never have lost him."

The heartbreak in his voice is my tipping point. I close the distance between us and take his hands in mine, bringing them to my lap. As I do, Wyatt lets out a shaky laugh and threads our fingers together.

"Needless to say, the answer was no, and the message was clear. That fucking cliché, is it better to have loved and lost than never loved at all? That was written for me and you, baby. Because the truth is, I can't stand not having you in my life, even if I am terrified of losing you."

"You were never in any danger of losing me, Wyatt," I interrupt. "I had an asthma attack. Not cancer. I've lived with this disease my entire life, and will continue to do so for the rest of it. Sometimes it is well controlled, and other times it isn't. But I am in no danger of dying from it, I promise."

He gives me a half smile that is not entirely reassuring. "There's more. It's not just the fear of losing you, it's the fear of putting you through the pain of losing me. My chance of getting the same cancer that took Ryder and my grandmother is significantly higher. I could get sick any time, and I don't know if I would survive. They didn't."

"I was raised by parents who were constantly terrified for me and of my disease. And it suffocated me. I refuse to live my own life in fear of *maybes* and *what ifs*." I sit up taller, strengthening my resolve. If this is what has been holding him back, then he needs to know how I feel. "Wyatt, I fell in love with you. And then you left. Knowing you are out there, and choosing not to be with me, hurts far more than the remote possibility of you getting sick one day. Life is never a guarantee, but I would far rather live mine with you in it than without."

His lips crash into mine before I can say another word, and I let myself be pushed back against the arm of the couch as his warm weight comes over me. Kissing him is like facing the sun after being in dark shadows. It's blinding, but warm and comforting at the same time.

"I couldn't choose not being with you. Not without destroying a part of me. You're my goddamn atmosphere, Paige. I need you to breathe."

This time, my kiss finds him first. As I press my hands into his back, needing him as close as possible, I feel, more than hear, his groan of desire. "Baby, stop. I need to worship you properly and I can't do that on a couch." I feel the absence of his body when he lifts off of me, and an actual whimper escapes me. Wyatt holds his hand out and I take it, letting him pull me to stand and straight into his arms. When I slide my hands around his upper body, I see him wince and freeze. Wyatt's face turns bashful and I cock my head to one side, confused by his reaction.

"I did some reading this week. You're right, E. Peake is a talented writer. But here's the thing. Your tattoo is missing the most important part of that line."

He lifts his shirt, and I gasp. My fingers reach out and gently trace the words tattooed on his side, in the same position as mine, as I whisper them in awe, "Till I was loved by you."

"I never knew love either, until you. I'm so sorry, Paige. I wasn't the man you deserve, I failed you and left when you needed me the most." His head hangs down, and I ache to tilt his chin back up so I can see his face. "I've realized just how selfish

I've been, about a lot of things. And I don't know if I can ever earn your forgiveness for that, but you need to know that you have my heart, and you always will. I just hope I still have yours."

I tear my eyes away from the words that complete the line on my side. "You do, Wyatt. You have it and you always will."

Hours later, after Wyatt reminds me exactly why orgasms are as wonderful and amazing as all of my friends claim, we lay in my bed, our naked bodies tangled together. He is lazily playing with my hair, twisting it around his fingers as my head rests on his chest.

The last thing I want to do is disturb the pure happiness emanating from us both, but there is one more answer I need from Wyatt.

"Why did you lie about who you really are and why you came to Dogwood Cove?"

His hand stills on my head for a beat, and his chest rises and falls under my cheek several times before he answers.

"There are a few answers to that question. Mostly because I didn't want to be me. I didn't want to be Wyatt Crawford. I wanted to just be a guy who could live the life he wants to live, instead of the one he feels guilted into living."

"And the life you want to live — that's what, exactly?" I ask cautiously.

"Not working for Crawford Books. The outdoor tour company was a real idea, something that Ryder and I dreamt up when we were younger. We had a whole plan to share a building, him running Crawford Books upstairs and me running WR Tours downstairs. Beachfront, of course."

"And the other reasons?"

Wyatt lets out a small huff. "You're gonna think I'm stupid. I was worried you wouldn't want to talk to me if you knew I was a Crawford. You know, us being the competition and all? I guess I didn't want to scare you away."

I slap his chest gently. "You're right, that is stupid."

We both laugh, then fall silent again. His hand starts stroking my hair once more, and it would be so soothing if I didn't feel the tension he's holding in his body underneath me. As much as I desperately want to know what he's thinking, I stay quiet, giving him the space he clearly needs.

"I want to stay here. In Dogwood Cove." His head shifts to the side so he's looking down at me "As long as I'm welcome."

"Of course you're welcome," I answer quickly, earning a smile.

"You sure Ethan and the guys won't show up to beat the shit out of me for leaving?"

I fight to hide my smirk but it breaks free. "I can't promise anything, but I will fight them back as much as I can."

"My knight in shining armour." Wyatt chuckles. "Wait, what is a female knight called?"

I lift my head and glare. "A knight."

Wyatt flips over so he's hovering above me, propped up on his elbows, which frame my face. His head dips down and he kisses the end of my nose. Even without my glasses on, at this close distance, I can see him clearly. "In case it wasn't clear, I want to stay in Dogwood Cove, with you. I love you, Paige Millstone."

Hearing those words from the one man for whom I have ever felt the same way feels as if a part of me that was missing has finally come home.

"I love you, too. And I would *love* it if you stayed."

"Good. I was thinking of taking Summer up on her offer to work together on the tourism company."

I lift a finger to his lips. "Wyatt, could we please put conversations about our friends and work aside for the time being? We've just expressed our love for each other for the first time. I do believe there are more appropriate ways to commemorate the moment."

Lust fills his dark eyes, lighting them on fire from within.

"I couldn't agree more."

CHAPTER TWENTY-FIVE

Resisting the urge to jump up and down like a little kid, I walk swiftly down the steps of city hall, permits tightly gripped in my hands. It's official, Ethan handed them over himself with a smile. WR Tours is opening later this spring, with our office based out at Oceanside Resort.

Now the fun begins. I've got a long list of equipment to purchase, staff to hire, a marketing plan to establish. But first, I need to find one very important person to celebrate with.

Paige closed the store early today for inventory. I promised to come by when I finished all of my work, bring some dinner, and help her.

But dinner will have to wait.

Using the key she gave me a couple of weeks ago, I open the door to Pages and walk in, closing and locking it behind me.

"Wyatt? I assume that's you?" Her slightly muffled voice comes from the back of the store, over where the new sitting area is set up.

"Yeah, baby. It's me." I make my way around the stacks of books that cover the floor. Soft instrumental music is playing, Paige's first choice when she needs background noise but still wants to focus and not be tempted to dance. The fact that I'm the only person she ever lets loose around, and shows her sensual side to, means almost as much as the three little words we can't stop saying to each other. She's turned me into a complete romantic fool, and I couldn't be happier.

Her head pops up from the floor in front of the couch. Hair sticks out every direction and her glasses are crooked. I don't bother to hide my grin as she stands up and walks over to me.

"You seem extremely cheerful. Did something happen?" I see the moment she remembers the significance of today as she claps her hands together. "You got all of the permits didn't you?"

"I did." I take her by the hips and gently start pushing her backwards until her legs hit the edge of the couch.

"What are you doing?"

Every now and then, Paige's lack of sexual experience shows, and she's oblivious to my attempts at seducing her. That's okay, though, because nothing gets her going faster than when I tell her, bluntly, what I have planned.

"I was thinking of stripping off your clothes and burying my face between your legs. Make you come a couple times with my tongue and my fingers before trying out some new positions on the couch."

"Oh...oh-okay," she stutters, dropping down onto the couch. I sink to my knees and pull her forward so I can kiss her lips, then mark a path with my mouth down her neck and across her bare shoulders. God, I love it when she wears tank tops. Easy access to so much more skin.

I pull back and peel her shirt up and over her head, then push her gently so she's leaning against the back of the couch. Unbidden, she lifts her hips, and I slide her leggings and underwear down and throw them behind me, then let my hands slowly creep back up her legs, generating shivers everywhere I touch.

"Have I told you how hot it is to see your body respond to my touch?"

Her answer is a moan when I lower my head and lick a path up her inner thighs. Her smell is intoxicating and I know from personal experience that her taste is even better. My mouth reaches my destination and I latch on to her clit and suck, hard.

"Wyatt!"

Her hands grab my head, but there's no need. I'm not going anywhere. I lick up her seam, lapping up all of her sweetness as she starts to writhe under me. I snake one arm up and place it across her hips, holding her in place as I continue to lick, suck, and devour her. Within moments she's crying out and her body convulses around my tongue. She's mid-shudder when I thrust two fingers in deep, earning another shriek.

"Oh God, I can't. Wyatt...p-please!"

"I've got you, baby. Always," I growl, then I give her what she needs, flicking her clit with my tongue and sending her catapulting into the stars for a second time. I could watch Paige climax for hours and never get sick of the sight. Her flushed cheeks, long lashes fluttering against her cheeks, parted lips; she's perfection.

I stand and quickly take off my clothes before settling onto the couch and lifting a pliant Paige onto my lap. She reaches behind and unsnaps her bra, and as soon as her breasts are free, my mouth is there, peppering her skin with open-mouthed kisses. I make my way over to one nipple and tease it with my tongue until it's a stiff nub, then move over to do the same on the other side. She's already wet from her first two orgasms, but nothing gets her ready faster than nipple play. And since there's no lube close at hand, I want her dripping with need. Paige's hips start to rock back and forth over my cock, then she snakes her hand in between us and wraps her fingers around my base and starts to stroke.

"Fuck. Paige," I say hoarsely, releasing her nipple and letting my head fall back. Her lips find my neck and she doesn't let up, rocking her heat over my length. It's an overload of sensation, and yet, still not enough all at once. I'll never have enough of this woman. I grab her hips and hold her still. My eyes find hers, and the love that's shining back at me is my undoing.

"I love you," I whisper reverently. Then I guide her up and onto the tip of my dick, my piercing making her squirm, before letting her slowly lower herself fully. She went on birth control two weeks ago, and the first time I slid into her bare, I felt like I had died and gone to heaven. Ever since then, Paige has been fixated on experimenting with different positions to see how my piercing can hit her inner walls differently.

I have been fully on board with all of her experiments. And I meant what I told her earlier, I do want to try a few new things. I want her bent over the top of the couch while I take her from behind. I want to spoon her and touch every side of her from the inside. But right now, I want this. The woman I love above me, where I can use my hands and my lips, as well as my cock, to make her fly.

"I love you, Wyatt." Paige's head tilts back as she begins to move, her body undulating above me. I start to rock my hips up and down, and we find a rhythm that feels as natural as breathing. It doesn't take very long before I feel her walls clenching my dick tightly and I know without a doubt that she's climbing toward another orgasm. It blows my mind how quickly I can get her there and how often. For a woman who claimed she didn't see the point to sex, Paige has certainly proven herself wrong. I've never known a more sensual woman, who is sexy without even trying.

I want more of her. All of her. I surge up into sitting and wrap my arms around her, crushing her to my body. Somehow, she manages to get her legs around my body, and there's no space between us, no definition of where she ends and I begin. This is when she lets go, gives herself over to me, to us, and I fucking love it.

Our movement becomes frenzied, our bodies unanimously desperate to reach the peak.

"I'm close. So close," Paige cries out, her fingers clawing at my back. I draw her head to where I can kiss her, needing even more connection. Then I tilt my hips, just enough so that I know my piercing is hitting her exactly where I want it to.

With a keening moan into our kiss, she comes in a spectacular release. My own orgasm hits in waves seconds later, and I grunt out her name over and over again as my cock jerks into her, until I finally stop coming. When I eventually feel some control over my body again, I slowly twist so that I can lay down along the length of the couch, pulling Paige down on top of me. Our limbs tangle together in a sticky, sweaty mess and pure, happy relaxation infuses my every cell.

"And to think, I believed you were coming to help with inventory," Paige murmurs teasingly against my chest as she traces the outline of the Valkyrie on my chest. I squirm when she hits a ticklish spot and cover her hand with mine.

"That *was* the plan. But I can't help it if you're too goddamn tempting. Besides. We needed to celebrate."

She turns slightly to prop her head up on her hands. "There was never any doubt in my mind that you would get your permits. While I agree, it's exciting that your business strategy is moving ahead as planned, I'm afraid I don't quite see what there is to celebrate."

I chuckle. She's just gotta be the pragmatic one all the time. "Paige, my love, sometimes a guy just wants a reason to seduce his woman until she can't walk."

A small frown mars her forehead. "You never need a reason to be intimate with me, Wyatt, I assure you. I will almost always be receptive to your advances."

"*Almost* always?" I flip us over so that I'm on top. "Why not just always? Hmm? What would make you not receptive?" I ask in mock seriousness.

Paige runs her hands up the sides of my body and around my neck. "Wyatt."

"What?"

"It was just a figure of speech. If I say I will always want you, will you kiss me?"

The plaintive tone to her voice makes me smile. "Baby, I would kiss you no matter what."

So, I do. And I don't stop for a very long time.

Epilogue

Paige

Never in my wildest dreams could I have pictured this moment, walking through the large wooden doors of the famous Bodleian Library on the grounds of Oxford University in England. My eyes dance around, trying to take it all in. Row upon row of old texts and manuscripts, intricate artwork on the walls and ceiling, the high arches, the circular tower, it's all too much. I feel tears track down my cheeks as I give in to the awe-inspiring place I am standing in.

"What do you think?" Wyatt's arm snakes around my waist. I tilt my head up to look at him, and his thumb lifts to gently swipe away my tears.

"It's incredible."

His kiss is slow and sweet, but I feel it down to my toes. Even after we part, him with a wink and walking off to look at something the guide is describing, I feel the touch of his lips on mine. Every moment we are together, my love for him grows stronger. When he first proposed a trip to England, I was overwhelmed with trying to decide what to see and where to go. Allowing Wyatt to take over the planning was a blessing, and at the same time, incredibly challenging. Having lived my entire adult life in control of my actions and decisions, relinquishing that on something as monumental as my first trip outside the country was incredibly difficult. I know he was frustrated at times when I would try to intervene, or drop weighted suggestions, but eventually, my friends were able to convince me to back off and let him take the lead.

Now, in this moment, I'm so glad I did. Wyatt thought of everything. First class seats on the way over allowed us to travel in complete comfort. The hotels he chose were the perfect balance of luxury and authentic British experience. Private tours of various historical sites, including Shakespeare's Globe theater in London. And now this. Our final stop, Oxford University and the Bodleian Library, all because of one comment I made about wanting to see some of the famous libraries of the world.

"Paige, come and look at this."

Wyatt's excitement infuses the air, and I hurry over to where he's standing, looking at a glass case.

"Is that..." I gasp, barely believing this is real.

"Shakespeare's first folio," Wyatt whispers reverently. His love of literature almost rivals my own, making this trip incredibly special for us both.

After we ogle the Shakespeare texts for as long as they'll allow us to, we make our way through the rest of the library. The history surrounding us, all these magnificent texts that have seen so much more than we could ever fathom, it fills me with an indefinable sense of rightness. As if this was predestined to happen for me, for Wyatt, for us. All of the pain and struggles we have been through as individuals and together brought us to this moment. Standing on the steps of the most beautiful library I have ever seen, I know in my heart that this is it.

"Will you marry me, Wyatt?"

My hand claps over my mouth as shock registers on both my face and Wyatt's. I was not planning to ask him to marry me. Those potent words escape from a part of me that I had no control over, yet as soon as I said them, I know them to be the most true expression of my love.

"What?" Wyatt's eyes are wider than I have ever seen. "No. You can't say that." His hand runs through his hair as he steps away from me, and an icy chill starts to creep through my veins. He looks back at me, curses, and closes the distance between us, immediately kissing me. "Get out of your head, baby. I love you. I want to marry you. I even have a fucking ring waiting for us back at the hotel."

"You do?" I manage to find my voice, blinking rapidly at him. I feel the chaotic swing of my emotions, from pure love, to abject terror in the face of his perceived rejection of my proposal, back to love. He chuckles and cups my face in his hands.

"Yes, you crazy woman. I was going to propose to you tomorrow at dinner. I had a whole plan in place, your friends helped me figure it all out."

I choke out a laugh as the realization hits me that my single most spontaneous action of my entire life ruined his careful planning. "I would say I'm sorry, but I am afraid I'm not. You helped me unleash my capacity to love and feel passion, and that's what I'm doing. I'm showing you my love and my passion and my unending desire to be with you for the rest of my life."

Wyatt pulls me into his arms, and my hands come up to rest on his chest. "Paige, I want nothing more than to be with you for the rest of our lives. You are both the most tempting woman I've ever met, and the truest love I never expected to find."

I lift up onto my toes and kiss him deeply. But his hands move to my waist and he gently sets me down.

"But if you think you're going to deprive me of proposing to the love of my life, you are wrong."

I smile cheekily up at him, my heart bursting with more love than I ever thought possible.

"You can propose, on two conditions. First, as long as you accept *my* proposal. And second, as long as you remember, I asked you first."

Wyatt's eyes are shining. For a man whose heart was so closed off for so long, he is full of emotion and love. "First, of course I accept. And second, I don't think I'll ever forget this moment."

This time our kiss is sweet, a promise of a future filled with more love than I ever imagined possible.

"I love you," he murmurs against my lips.

"And I love you."

And there, surrounded by literary history, my future begins.

Desperate for more Paige and Wyatt?
Read their extended epilogue by visiting
https://bit.ly/JuliaJarrett_TT_bonus

ACKNOWLEDGMENTS

This particular book would not have happened without several people. Dana, for keeping me sane and pushing me when I wanted to stop. Carolina, for keeping me organized and on task with the hundred other things I was juggling. Erica for reassuring me over and over that Paige was the way she needed to be.

As always, my support network of family and friends were indispensable. My kids and husband, thank you for putting up with my crazy hours, mood swings, and wild stress. My KKSB sisters, for being my rocks through everything, editor Chris, assistant Carolina, beta readers Erin and Erica. It takes a true village to do this job and I love mine.

And, thank you to you dear reader. You keep me going, with your words of support and praise. I never could have imagined this life for myself, but I am beyond thrilled to keep bringing you stories.

ALSO BY JULIA JARRETT

Dogwood Cove

Always and Forever

Rumours and Romance

Work and Play

Truth and Temptation

Then and Now

Passion and Promises: A Dogwood Cove Novella Collection

The Donnellys of Dogwood Cove

Dare To Kiss you

Hate To Want You

Pretend To Love You

Promise To Marry You

Dare To Marry You: A Donnellys of Dogwood Cove Holiday

Novella

One Night To Win You

Standalone

Seductive Swimmer - A standalone novel set in the Cocky Hero World, inspired by Vi Keeland and Penelope Ward's Cocky Bastard series

About Julia Jarrett

Julia Jarrett is a busy mother of two boys, a happy wife to her real-life book boyfriend and the owner of two rescue dogs, one from Guatemala and another one from Taiwan. She lives on the West Coast of Canada and when she isn't writing contemporary romance novels full of relatable heroines and swoon-worthy heroes, she's probably drinking tea (or wine) and reading.

<u>Follow Julia:</u>

Instagram

Facebook: Julia Jarrett's Nutty Muffins

TikTok

BookBub

Goodreads